W9-ARH-643

BLUE HILL AVENUE

BLUE HILL

THE BOBBS • MERRILL COMPANY, INC.

AVENUE

A Novel by

MARK MIRSKY

INDIANAPOLIS AND NEW YORK

Simcha appeared in *Ararat,* Spring, 1966,
and was reprinted in *The Single Voice*
and *Metro Boston.* Excerpts from
"A Consolation" and "A Complication"
appeared in *Partisan Review,* No. 3, 1971.

The Bobbs-Merrill Company, Inc.
Indianapolis • New York

Library of Congress Catalogue Card Number 73-173205
Manufactured in the United States of America

To my grandfather
ISRAEL MIRSKY

CONTENTS

BLUE HILL AVENUE

INTRODUCTION

A MAN in late middle age, a crack in the center of his brow, as if it has been stamped on, split in two, stares at me. Cigarette ashes, crumbling stars, on his coat collar. And the cloth of his old tweed shaker is patched with strips of black masking tape which run scars through the garment. There are spots of red paint on the face. A pine board a foot wide nailed across his belly. "EGG" in faint gold paint is lettered on a shapeless gray homburg, the last letter stretching off the brim, held only by a ribbon of that black tape.

The details shift. Now the tape holds an ear to the face; a pool of blood appears at the mouth. The coat is whole again. The board is nailed to the heart. And "EGG" has fallen off the hat.

The glass is shattered. He has moved an inch. The pane so dusty, the specks coat it in the silver backing of a mirror. Even this window, sacrosanct, one of the last to go. The store has been broken into.

The tiny row of shops is nothing but blank panes of plywood, this, the last that still holds on to a view of the street. They say that the door is unlocked at times. A shadow moves in and out. Rumors, ah, they stir inside.

The egg store ran right to the end. Cockeyed, the owner, told his friends in the back of the synagogue, sell, get out, before it's too late. Yet business was better than ever for him. He thought. They even bought some of his eggs, an article he hadn't moved for forty years.

Maybe that's why he had his head cracked on the sidewalk one morning, brains spilling out like yolk.

Next door to his store not even glass. The boards nail the shop tight as a coffin. It's a mess inside, unusable. The engines got here just in time. A year or two ago. The whole block would have gone. In the gutted ruin they found a charred corpse. A bum, someone who had crept in out of the fierce cold which can bite you to death on the avenue in February ice. A copy of Spinoza, half charcoal, was lying beside him, also the remains of a large laundry bag stuffed with smoldering socks. He must have been using it as a bed and fallen asleep smoking a scavenged cigarette butt. That's what the coroner imagined. The remains could not be identified. Although the owner had a suspicion.

The landlord of these stores used to be president of our *shul*. A local magnate of the avenue, this business has pinched him hard. His stores aren't worth much now. He can hardly give them away to the blacks coming in. His holdings up and down the thoroughfare are a liability. He wants to shake loose of the taxes. Cursed as if by a devil, his fire insurance has been canceled. The flames drive him toward bankruptcy.

At least this row is still standing. Down the avenue the bones are sticking out all over, scorched beams, the corpse of a burned-out shopping center. Black, white, fire knows no race, brotherhood, soul.

There are still a few left, cowering behind police locks, burglar alarms, heavy steel grilles, pretending to do business. The fruit store has a few rotten apples, an old pear, dried plums and in the back they take wagers on the last few digits of the Treasury balance, numbers racket. Yet it all seems furtive, desperate, beleaguered swapping, the last jerk of a chicken's wings, its throat slit. From top to bottom, Blue Hill Avenue lies under lock and key. Above Grove Hall to Mattapan Square stretches a steel grate, a bar, plywood.

As if the Jews had swept out of Dorchester in one blow. A thunderclap catastrophe the rabbi called upon our heads.

CHAPTER ONE

THE SMILE OF RABBI LUX

RABBI LUX of Dorchester lived in the shadow of his telephone. A man afraid of his telephone? Well, things are strange, this modern world.

Yet Lux was the leading rabbi of Dorchester. A scholar, a man of distinguished parts, why should he knot the black rubber of the telephone cord about his middle finger like a phylactery strap and groan—twisting his soul before God?

The sight of the rabbi so entangled with a phone would have caused dismay among his congregation. The pious of Boston would have been shocked. Down on his knees before a little black Mammon?

In the orthodox community of Greater Boston and throughout New England Rabbi Lux was known as a prince, a master of the Holy Word. His piety was a byword, a slogan. A mother in suburban Sharon who grew up in Dorchester would sweep her five-year-old's finger from the chocolate pudding, coo—"Grow up to be a Rabbi Lux."

Is it not a tradition that the scholars are princes among us? The crown of Torah is reckoned greater than the crown of royalty or priesthood. The very words of the Law are compared to vessels of gold. "The more you scour them and rub them, the more they glisten and reflect the face of him who looks at them." Did not Moses come down with beams of light from Mount Sinai, glowing in the brightness of the Law? As Rabbi Meir said, "Whosoever labors in the Law—the whole world is indebted to him." Rabbi Lux was owed. The Almighty himself might be beholden? A mystical doctrine says God exists only by recognition of the scholars.

So perhaps Rabbi Lux deserved the compliment. Increasingly he was paid in such. And he didn't get too many of them. The golden words had fewer and fewer takers.

In a half-empty synagogue Rabbi Lux presided. One or two old beards, middle-aged people whose hard luck kept them in the low-rent districts, children of recent immigrants—these were the only ones who regularly took seats.

In the midst of hardships Lux did not give way. He cut his own salary so the congregation could afford a young, mellow-voiced cantor. He was unfailingly available to give advice. And he never lost his temper.

For instance, when the cigarette holes were burned in the velvet wrappings of the Torah scrolls. Who was the culprit? The president of the congregation. The old man had been sneaking a smoke behind the sacred scrolls as he sat with them in his lap during the service. In the place of honor, beside the rabbi, up on the bema —with the rolls of the Law in his lap. He fell asleep to the droning of the chant and while dozing burned large holes through the nap of the cherry velvet Torah covering. Someone smelled smoke. "*Shmendrick!*" screamed the young cantor as he snatched the smoldering Law from the old president's lap. The parchment was about to go up in flames. "Shhhhhhhhhhh," begged Rabbi Lux. "Shhhhhhh . . . an accident . . . shhhhhhh . . . it's all right . . . shhhhh . . ."

Shhhhhh? You think it was just a rag he burned a hole in? You must know that among us Jews a Torah covering is a sacred article. Covered with jewelry and heavy brocade, we auction off the privilege of buying one. Why? A Torah covering is an accessory to the holiness of the Divine Word. You can't throw one out when the nap is worn down. It has to be stored away. Only for the gravest of purposes—a shroud for the stranger—can it be used.

A cloth that has embraced the holy body of Torah, has hugged and clung to that wisdom enwrapped in the Writ—such a garment has its own laws of respect. Only to touch the velvet as the scrolls are carried through the synagogue is an honor. The president was lucky he was at the head of an enlightened congregation. A century before he might have had stones thrown at him.

Shhhhhhh . . . Rabbi Lux had his wife stitch up the holes. The synagogue couldn't afford a new wrapping. The old president was touchy about being reminded. Don't force a man to dwell on mistakes. The president could have given a new wrapping. He didn't. He felt that he was already paying more than his share of synagogue costs. Mistakes. "Enough," said the rabbi. Shhhhh . . . it's fixed. Like new. Enough! There were enough troubles already. Don't dwell. Please . . . Shhhh.

Rabbi Lux was a scholar. He studied how to forgive. No matter how outrageous or blustering sin seemed when it first shoved itself into the study of Rabbi Lux, he refused to pass judgment. Another rabbi on being confronted with such and such a sin might have laid hands on and cast it from his thoughts. Ugly, malicious, diseased with self-justification—when one comes into your study to boast—kick it out the door!

Not so, Rabbi Lux. He would beckon just such a sin to a seat. "Make yourself comfortable." Then he would look at it for a while. Make small talk. "How's the weather?"

"Hot."

Rabbi Lux would sigh with sympathy. Yes, and probably the sin had a headache. They would talk about the flu and other illnesses going around the world. Soon the sin would be slumping in its seat. A bit of its arrogance, its cocksure bearing gone, a small voice begins to talk about how badly it was feeling lately. Pretty soon Rabbi Lux and the sin were discussing, diagnosing, and making suggestions about alleviating its condition.

After such a discussion, the sin in the heart of the president of the congregation decided to give up cigarettes. The president still refused to discuss paying for a new Torah covering. The cantor of the synagogue had threatened to resign if it wasn't paid for. But he let himself be mollified by an increase in pay. Where it came from? Rabbi Lux always tried to meet a sin halfway.

Rabbi Lux tried to hold a dialogue of understanding with each and every act of evil that came to him. When he said to the sin, "Make yourself comfortable," or "Make yourself at home," he wasn't being rhetorical. He actually tried to take the sin into his own heart, to absorb some of its evil in his own system. In this dialogue of compassion, he did not keep at a distance from the sin but rather he invited it to come close.

Sins!

They have a bad smell. Try to swallow one! Some men get sick at heart over evil. Rabbi Lux got sick in the stomach and bowels.

It seemed as if in the case of impacted evildoers only Rabbi Lux could purge them. I remember when they brought the rabbi to the Charles Street Jail to speak with Yitzchock Meladnick the Safe Khnocker.

Meladnick! At the age of eight he got into the safe at our Hebrew school. A child prodigy who started out in his chosen career by shaking down relatives in the garment district. Our Yitzchock went through half the strongboxes of Boston, had bastards everywhere and slung lead with abandon too.

It was a pleasure to our Dorchester community to see at least one Jewish face in with all the Irish and Italian hoods in the city. Itzy in the hands of the Suffolk County sheriff. Itzy being drawn by the state police. Itzy between the arms of two burly F.B.I. men. If he had kept going, well, he might have rubbed shoulders with J. Edgar Hoover and said, "*Vas toutsta?*" to the Supreme Court. Always a nice smile too. He wept tears when they finally convicted him. He cried for the rabbi.

After that interview the rabbi didn't come out of the bathroom for a week, a permanent strain on his bowels.

Sins are egotistical. Not only did they take up the rabbi's time, they never thought, "Rabbi Lux is the leader of a poor congregation—maybe I should leave a contribution."

Meladnick the Safe Khnocker didn't. And he went to jail, a wealthy man. With grief, trouble, and evil deeds, people pestered Rabbi Lux all day. His scholarship in the Talmud was constantly interrupted. Finally he had to curtail duties at the synagogue to give attention to these people. Yet Rabbi Lux remained patient.

From the Talmud every morning, he lifted the mantle of the benevolent Hillel. He cultivated a warm and understanding smile. His disposition was to be a pleasant garden. He watered it constantly with injunctions to mercy and forgiveness toward his fellow man. And on his lips there grew a smile so sweet that those who tasted of it would often find a cloying melancholy in their mouths. Such sweetness could only arise from a terrible sadness. What rank, decaying soil was this smile nurtured in? All the sins that Rabbi Lux had swallowed?

I ask this question but most of the rabbi's congregation did not. They crowded into his study, seeking the ripened fruits of his counsel. They tore away what they needed, dropped their evil-smelling sins, and went home. All day long they trampled on his time. Not just in the synagogue, but on his way to and from *shul,* the rabbi was assaulted. His progress down Blue Hill Avenue toward his *shul* a caravan. Every shopkeeper and customer on the avenue stopped business and ran up to him. And if they didn't have a problem, they manufactured one—just to be able to get a taste of that halvah of honey and nuts, the smile of Rabbi Lux.

CHAPTER TWO

THE EDUCATION OF YEHOODISS—I

EVERY vineyard has its keeper. At night the vineyard of Rabbi Lux was guarded by the bulk of his wife, Yehoodiss. The crowd of petitioners might follow the rabbi right onto his porch. Tumbling into the tiny front hall of the three-family house which sheltered his rooms on its top floor, they might ascend a step or two of the creaking, broken stairs. But there they were stopped, 200 pounds, Yehoodiss. Not merely stopped—pushed right down the stairs, off the porch, into the street.

"Not tonight, *nu!* Not tonight!" she shouted in her high-pitched voice. "Enough! Enough!" she screamed, punching faces. She threw herself into their midst from the top of the stairs. Wielding a clenched fist, cleared the hall, porch, and street of petitioners.

And when, on the way back, she found one still clinging to the rabbi's good nature, having buttonholed Lux and forced him to listen to a fresh woe under the stairwell—Yehoodiss gave him a look—Dracula. The man's neck muscles tightened. A chill to the base of his spine. The skin of his back crept together, raisin flesh. Yehoodiss spoke with acid sweetness. "You'll see him tomorrow. Not tonight! Not tonight!" she repeated as she tugged Lux up the stairs.

No matter how great the crowd following him or how pressing matters at the synagogue, Rabbi Lux always came home on time. At the beginning of his marriage he came late a few times. Yehoodiss went to get him.

The first time she caused a scene in the synagogue. In front of the janitor, the cantor, the president of the *shul.* She tore her hair. Her blouse. Cried. Screamed. She had fits up and down the aisle. The rabbi, bolting out of his study, found his wife, her breasts exposed, lying on the synagogue floor, chewing on mouthfuls of the dirty red rug.

They bundled her up in old prayer shawls and laid her down on one of the hard wooden pews. It was just before sundown on Friday evening. *Erev shabbes!* Finally she calmed down and went to sleep. The sun had already disappeared. You can't ride on the Sabbath—no ambulance. Yehoodiss had to be carried home on the shoulders of the president, the *shummus,* the cantor, and someone who had wandered in off the street when the screaming began.

They took the back streets rather than the avenue to get to the rabbi's house. But at that hour of evening shadows everyone is out on the front porches of their wooden tenements. Don't think they didn't stare and gape. Rabbi Lux alone would have attracted attention, shaking as he walked, turning right and left, his finger to his lips, whispering loudly, Shhh . . . shhhh. . . .

A miracle—quiet. A profound silence on the 15 streets that the party took to get Mrs. Lux home. Hundreds of people crowded noiseless onto the porches and into the street to get a look. Another miracle that the fragile landings didn't collapse, cripples, invalids, babies, men in shirt sleeves, women in their nighties: the alleys filling up. Only one dog disturbed the hush that fell on these usually raucous blocks. One dog that seemed to be possessed followed behind the procession, yapping and barking at the heels of Rabbi Lux. And every time the rabbi turned to it and implored, prayed, Shhhhh . . . shhhhh . . . it howled louder.

Rabbi Lux was taught never to come home late. To disentangle himself no matter how terrible a sin he was involved in and hurry his steps to the young bride who awaited him, sitting alone in their four empty rooms on the top floor of a wooden three-family.

Yehoodiss learned to relax her fierce hug. If you meet your husband accidentally, in the fruit man's, you don't grab him. A man is not a tomato to be squeezed and squeezed until you are sure there are no rotten spots. Slowly the shoppers would stop pinching the peaches and apricots and watch Yehoodiss.

One day I was at the corner of Wellington standing over the lemons, looking for sour ones, when the rabbi walked through the door. He had come in to buy a box of dates. Yehoodiss looked up, scooped him up in the middle of the store as he was asking the price.

At this time Yehoodiss was young, plump. Her flesh ripened on her body, a plum. One could hardly resist a pinch. In Yiddish the old men mumbled—a *zaftig maidle.*

The beauty of Rabbi Lux was less palpable. A small man, a bit fat, his skin was pale like the underbelly of an animal. A white that had been cultivated in the light of countless candles through the line of Lithuanian rabbis and scholars who were Rabbi Lux's ancestors. And from the strange white skin of his face, from that suddenly exposed white, shone two eyes, dark and brown, shying at the world.

Yehoodiss took hold of her surprised husband with short, powerful arms. Reaching up, she embraced him, pushing Lux back into the cucumbers. His elbow sank into a box of strawberries. She nuzzled him. Her hair brushed against his smooth-shaven face. Her fingers found the loose nape at the back of his neck and squeezed. Even the cantaloupe pokers stopped their business after a minute of Yehoodiss' hold and stared. The fruit man's scales swung empty. The fruit man, his apron stained with the blood of berries, looked on. The woman was half crazy. Still, if his wife bit into him some day, juicy nectarine? Who can weigh?

The rabbi was smothered. A man is not a bag of oranges. His breath was spent. He was in danger of having the seeds popped out.

"A gift, a gift," he gasped. In the midst of her squeezes and little grunts his wife heard him. "A gift, a gift!" She drew back.

In his hand, an empty box of dates. The cellophane had burst open in the press of Mrs. Lux's clutch. The dates spilled out onto his black rabbinical suit in sweet and sticky clusters. A few of the cloying brown fruits crushed against Yehoodiss' summer dress of cream white. As Rabbi Lux pulled away, the dates clung to the pale cloth. One, in the center of a large brown stain on the left side of her bosom, shone in the sunny fruit store.

Rabbi Lux leaned forward and kissed his wife. "It will come out at the cleaner's," he stated. And picking a date off his suit, he offered it to her.

Yehoodiss began to believe that Rabbi Lux was not going to run away. He seemed to pass tests. The week she insisted she was sick and he had to stay by her bed 24 hours or else. It was on the High Holidays, on Yom

Kippur. Yes, kneeling by her pillow, Rabbi Lux had to begin the service, opening up with the Kol Nidre, "All vows, bonds, promises . . . oaths, they shall be annulled."

When Yehoodiss heard that she almost passed away. Maybe she wasn't well. When the rabbi chanted the list of sins, she groaned, talking half of them to heart. "Forgive us for the sin of our own will, the sin of hardening our hearts, the unknowing sin, the sin of presumption, for confusion of mind. Forgive us! Pardon us! Grant us atonement!" The furniture shook with her cries.

In the synagogue they were in a fever. Where was the rabbi? What was going on? This was the night they raised money for the year. The *shummus* went through the audience and the president announced donations he had buttonholed for the Torah and book fund, the Hebrew school, the building improvements, even the rabbi's salary. It was the most important service. Beth Rachmoniss stood or fell on it. And the principal attraction of the fund raising was missing? Who wanted to parade his charity just for the *shummus* and the congregation? The big givers, the little ones too, wanted to show the rabbi how generous they could be.

The officers of the synagogue, their followers, came and banged on Lux's door. "Open the gates of the Temple!" begging him to come out. The rabbi, in a sweat inside, rocked back and forth singing, "For all this, forgive us! Pardon us! Grant atonement!" But he didn't leave. The gates of the Lux house stayed shut.

The rabbi's synagogue the next day was a vessel filled with confusion. The rabbi was not there to pray for them. The voice of mercy was missing in the synagogue. How harsh the accusations they had to sing sounded without his voice among them.

We are insolent . . . we are obstinate
We have trespassed, we have dealt treacherously,

We have spoken slander, we have acted perversely,
And we have wrought wickedness, we have done
Violence, framed lies, counseled evil, scoffed,
Revolted . . . committed whoredom.

As if people weren't sick enough from fasting.

Stories went back and forth while they begged, "for the sin we have committed before you by ensnaring our neighbor," and the wails of guilt, "for the sin we have committed before you by talebearing," as they tried to figure out what was going on in the rabbi's house.

It was an awful service for Lux to miss. We have no confession in the synagogue. Yom Kippur is the only time the congregation can unburden itself of guilt. So heavy does the weight of sin become in the room that it can't be lifted off a man's back by himself. The whole community has to get together and help each other shoulder. All together and for one another, we cry, "For the sake of Abraham, Isaac, Jacob, Moses, etc., deal kindly with *us,* renew us into a good year, annul the evil decree."

How the community berated Rabbi Lux all year for his absence. They bent his ear back and forth with Why, why? All he would answer—there was sickness in the house.

Yet Yehoodiss' grip was relaxing. She no longer insisted that the rabbi sit at the table long after supper was over, sit and stare at her with undivided attention until it was time for bed.

Rabbi Lux suffered without complaining. Suffered without speaking. One of the rules Yehoodiss had laid down for these sessions—she would do most of the talking. So when she stopped chattering there was often a long silence. Rabbi Lux was then allowed to prompt her —a short question. This would usually start a flow of associations in her mind, a shallow basin, talk quickly tumbled out. Talk overflowed and spilled across the table, lapped around the seat of recumbent Rabbi Lux.

What did she talk about? Scraps and bits of nothing. "Who was that woman in the fruit store crying? The tangerines were wet from it. They were damp in the bag. In the egg store, two or three in tears. Always! That old man, that's in there all the time. What's with him? On Morton Street, I saw him writing down numbers. You know on Morton Street that discount den, who is it, Hot Shot's? He's a hot shot, what's he do that's so hot? I looked in the window and it's all cheap stuff. I wouldn't want it in my house. A new piece or two, though. Too old, that's the trouble with this furniture. What's the matter with the president of the *shul?* He's been getting red in the face. He should take Alka-Seltzer. A good burp! Who was the little boy with pimples who burped when the chazan made the blessing? His mother kept pinching him. She shouldn't so hard. She has a pimple on her lip. From pinching? Shouldn't do it. It won't go away. I got a pimple once. It stayed for a month. I had to go to the hospital."

Rabbi Lux looked up at Yehoodiss and smiled. He watched his wife relax as she talked on and on, sure of his attention.

And so Yehoodiss learned. She let him bring a book to the table. She let him read while she talked. Finally Rabbi Lux was permitted to retire into his study about an hour after the meal. All that was required of him was that occasionally, in the midst of a difficult footnote, he would relax his mind by listening to the torrent of conversation that flowed through the open door of the study from the kitchen. He would wait until the pause occurred, ask a question, listen to the waters renew themselves and then go peacefully back to the quiet pools of Rashi's speculation.

CHAPTER THREE

THE EDUCATION OF YEHOODISS—II

GRADUALLY homely patterns established themselves. At first the neighbors complained. The sound of Yehoodiss throwing herself across the room upon the rabbi, knocking over tables, chairs, overturning couches, toppling onto the floor, made the house tremble. Through the windows one heard shrieks, shouts. Now she began to restrain herself. She began to understand Rabbi Lux was important in this business. She didn't strongarm him the moment he touched the mattress, she waited in her bed, half-asleep, confident his timid hand would touch her.

So the Lux family became almost conventional. The rabbi came home from synagogue. They ate supper. Yehoodiss began to mend clothes and knit while she talked. And the rabbi continued to listen while he studied.

Yehoodiss decided after a few years of these settled habits to take a more active part in the rabbi's life. Go out and assume the duties of a rabbi's wife.

She had begun to get headaches. They cleared up as soon as Rabbi Lux came home, but in the long spaces of afternoon when he was away, a head pain talking to oneself. And silence made her head ache worse than anything.

It was a rare afternoon when Rabbi Lux could steal out of his *shul* and run home early to his wife. Twice a month, maybe.

Scream, take a fit, collapse in the aisle, regardless, Yehoodiss couldn't sit next to her husband or follow him up to the altar. Like it or not, she was forced to take a seat among the women. She had to spend her fury within the sisterhood of Congregation Beth Rachmoniss.

Still, Beth Rachmoniss didn't have an ordinary sisterhood. The personality of Rabbi Lux distilled itself into the sweet cup that Beth Rachmoniss sipped. They didn't just sit around and gossip, give jumbo benefits for the benefit of their own benefit. The endless cakes and cookies that they baked for the welfare of the synagogue's meager treasury, these cakes and cookies did not melt entirely in their own mouths.

They went to the state mental hospital. Waited by the beds of the patients, spooning out a broth of chicken and rice. A special recipe from the old country. "It's a cure," ladling it into the mouth of a spastic.

To the veteran's hospital to leave cakes with pink frostings and a white Star of David on the beds of the amputees. They left them regardless of the soldier's race, religion, color, or country of origin. Every bed counted as a good deed, said Rabbi Lux. His congregation obeyed. "I'm doing a good deed—a *mitzvah,*" an old lady would explain as she gingerly put down a large piece of chocolate cake with a silver Mogen David on the bed of an armless colored serviceman. "A good deed," she said apprehensive, "so don't throw stones in Roxbury!" And hobbled to the next.

At Passover the sisterhood distributed baskets of matzoh and wine to the needy. At Purim children came from blocks upon blocks, crowding into the basement banquet hall to get free pastries. The little ones ate themselves sick on *choomentashen*—triangles of dough stuffed with prunes. They filled their pockets with cones of crackers that had been soaked and hardened in a paste of walnuts and honey. Sisterhood Beth Rachmoniss distributed sweetness.

Yet the sisterhood did not merely give away cakes.

You know, in our community, when troubles come down on a man or woman's head, they don't usually take to the bottle. Let South Boston drink their troubles under the table. Let them stagger about red-faced, spilling out woe like urine, making a bed in a pile of beer cans.

Yet maybe better to pour out woe quickly. Why bottle it up deep inside where it turns to vinegar? From this comes stomach upsets, indigestion, finally the stomach lining cracks, old leather, you wake up with an ulcer.

Our women stopper their grief within. They store it away in the pantries of their hearts. The grief of an old lady from our part of Dorchester is terrible. Once she starts pouring from the bottles, once she takes them off the shelf and begins to fill your cup—you may sit there for years.

To such homes by instinct Sisterhood Beth Rachmoniss would go. A sweet cookie to alleviate a bitter draught.

Yehoodiss Lux made friends among the sisterhood. Rabbi Lux smiled on her participation and so Yehoodiss began to go out with her new familiars. She too began to sugar the community.

Tongues wiggled like pickles in brine. They watched her with satisfaction.

Why? Why should anyone in Dorchester be bitter toward the wife of our beloved rabbi? Ah, the truth, there were people in our community who resented the rabbi. Jacob Blatz, the sock man, for instance. A poor fellow who used to be around the avenue. A businessman of sorts, one who went bankrupt about a month or two after he scraped together enough money to open a store. Four or five times this happened. Not enough customers came in to buy his stock of socks. They were cheaply made and he charged too much.

Jacob Blatz was a *shmendrick*, a tribe whose members we don't lack for in our Jewish nation. He was a fool and yet he was nasty. You couldn't tell him anything. He bought bad lots of socks, with holes in them and weak heels. And he paid twice what he had to. He was such a big mouth to the wholesalers, so arrogant and overbearing, that they didn't scruple to cheat him. He shouted at customers when they asked questions, gave out the wrong sizes and matched socks of different colors. When his credit finally gave out, he sat on the curb opposite the G & G Delicatessen and tried to sell old pairs out of a cardboard box. I think he threw his own socks into the box. Because he didn't wear any. Who would buy hosiery from such a creature?

He threw himself, his wife and his little one on the synagogue. Jewish Welfare supported him. And he borrowed money. The only one who would lend it to him was Rabbi Lux. You think Jacob was grateful? He began to insult the rabbi. He called him a fool. When Jacob Blatz's last store went bankrupt, he became an atheist. He used to go to the rabbi's study to argue. After getting a five-dollar bill out of Lux, he would sneer and ask, "How can you be a rabbi? There was no justice in the world, no mercy! The whole thing is a fake. A man can do anything, no one cares. You can rob or murder, just don't get caught."

The rabbi was perplexed. He rubbed his forehead.

Jacob made filthy noises in his face. Hours of the rabbi's time he took, then went off to call Lux a simpleton. "That nincompoop!" he laughed to his listeners along the avenue. "What does he know about anything? Mumbles in Hebrew. Collects money for nothing. A bug."

Jacob! For a year he dragged the rabbi's good name along the gutter with him. One day he ran off, leaving his wife and child behind.

Yet he left plenty behind with dirty words. Why was there so much malice toward the rabbi? A sweet and timid man.

There are people who want to be slapped. If someone had said to Menshivick the Book, "Stop it! Go back and be a C.P.A.!" If someone had told the ladies whose hair was glittering gold, "You look like Jezebel. A painted whore!"

There are those who want their rabbi to come with a big stick, shake it over their head and shout.

Lux was a little too good, too pious, for much of Dorchester.

Much of Dorchester had written unofficial amendments, bylaws, codicils, to the Ten Commandments their ancestors had accepted at Sinai. They would have preferred a rabbi who knew a trick or two himself. They would have felt more at home. That smile of Lux's made one too self-conscious. Better to have a rabbi one could clap on the back with a hearty "I know what you're up to!"

So many in the community, though not angry with the rabbi, were on the lookout for some slander of him so he could share in their misdeeds. And if not the rabbi, the rabbi's wife would do. They remembered Yehoodiss' funeral procession from the synagogue of a few years back—the dog at the distracted rabbi's heel. They began to speculate. Who was this Yehoodiss? Her origins and pedigree?

In the delicatessens of Dorchester over half-bitten sandwiches, tongues wagged. The mouths of the toothless watered over the gossip. One old lady suggested to a table cluttered with old men spilling tea over each other—"A *shicksa!* A *shicksa* from Beacon Hill, that's what!" But no, mumbles and grumbles rejected the suggestion. It was a little farfetched to imagine Yehoodiss Lux a non-Jewish girl from the society heights of Beacon Hill. Sharper teeth went to work on the tough question—where did Yehoodiss come from?

"From Winthrop!" an *alter kocker* suggested. "From right outside Boston. She was a nice Jewish girl and from Winthrop but the rabbi had made her pregnant!" A low murmur of satisfaction went round the table.

"So what happened to the baby?" a voice intoned sarcastically. There is always a cynic in the crowd. It was unthinkable, the only thing that could have happened to the baby. A chorus of guttural negatives drowned out the suggestion. It died before it had a chance to develop, to swell in the cups of the hangers on. The old men stirred the dregs of their coffee. Something better than that.

And yet—who knows? Even as they stirred silently, they thought—Behind that pious smile of Rabbi Lux, who knows? Spoons clattered against their empty cups and the talk at the table again became animated. "From Europe," came from a middle-aged peroxide blonde who had wedged a seat between two old men and was now chattering on, "From Europe. I'm not kiddin', just like my mother, just like her. She was just as nuts as this one. All arranged before! They bring her over. She never has to see the man. He never sees her. The parents do it. Prearranged."

"It's it!" came a cry. Menshivick, a bookie in the community, who had been quietly sitting at the table, taking the whole conversation in, jumped to his feet. "Listen!" Hopping with excitement. "I'll make book on it!" He got up, sat down, got up again. "I'll make a bet! I got it! I'll take a bet! I'll take it. At a thousand to one. I'll make it. *Oy vey! Oy vey!* It's it! It's it!"

Fifty voices came at him at once. "So what is it? So what? What is it? *Nu?* Tell us? Sit down! Stand up! You crazy? Tell us!"

"Crazy! Nuts!" he shouted over the din. "It's it!" And he collapsed in his chair and began to babble. "A thousand to one. I'll make the bet. I got it. I got it. It's it."

The voices screamed—"What, what?" And then they began to hush one another. "Shhhh, shhh . . ." "Let him speak." "Shhhh . . ." "What?" "Shhhh. . . ."

From Menshivick a torrent of words came pouring out like . . . like he had been chewing Feen-a-mint all day. Like a laxative had exploded inside him. His bottom burst and out it came. He ran at the mouth. "Nuts! Crazy! I'm telling you, she is crazy. How he met her? Believe me, in a nut house. She was crazy, he took pity. Right here in our Mattapan nut house. I'll make a bet. A softie. Lux is a softie. He's half-*meshugge* himself.

"He goes to visit, you know, once a week, the nut house. One day he comes in—she's lying down there. In a negligee I'll bet. *Nu!* With one of her breasts showing. Right there in the women's ward. Maybe she's a nut, but smart. One look at Lux and she knows—a softie. Right away she starts crying, not too loud, just enough. Lux is a softie. I'll bet she cried all over him. She saw him. She grabbed him. Her breasts fell out. *Nu,* right there in the women's ward on the bed."

And Menshivick leaned back, his eyes oozing tears of delight. "Butter! He's butter. Right on the bed she cries on him. She's hot on him. She grabs him. He's a softie this Luxie. He melts. And she gets better right away. She shoves her bubbies back in. She makes talk. She smiles. She's got him."

Menshivick leaned back further, exulting. "And that nut. He doesn't know any better. Heeee heeee heeee!"

The delicatessen filled with his cackle. His chair tottered on one leg. "Believe me. I'll make book on it. Heeee heeee heeee!"

He screeched, "They got married in the nut house!"

A crash, the old bookie's chair fell over. But too late. From out of his mouth those words had come and, though bad, they smelled like truth. They stunk right across Dorchester.

So, of course, it got back to Yehoodiss. When you climb the stairs of a tenement and the kids run down the hallway before you shouting, "Here comes the *meshuggeneh!*"—you know, people have been talking.

Yehoodiss could hear it also at Beth Rachmoniss. There was something in the air besides cookies and cakes. The women gathered in tight knots, whispering, pointing, breaking off their conversations when she approached. There was an ugly sound to the buzz that stopped and started again as she walked away. Yehoodiss stood in the middle of the room trying to catch something from the babble of the agitated circle around her.

A deaf old lady in the sisterhood hobbled up to her from one of the groups. "Listen," the old lady asked, "I couldn't hear from them. Who is it?" She bent toward Yehoodiss so she wouldn't miss the reply, "Who is the rabbi's wife in Dorchester who is *meshugge*?"

Yehoodiss did not have a fit. She stuffed a cookie in her mouth. She went home. She didn't explode before the rabbi. She said nothing to her husband. In the days that followed she went out less in the community. But she went out. She spent less time at the sisterhood. Yet she went to all the meetings. And there she picked a few special friends. And the extra time Yehoodiss now spent with them on the telephone.

CHAPTER FOUR

A SHORT DIGRESSION

CRAZY? My ears are ringing with that half-truth.

I knew Yehoodiss. She was born in Pinsk. When Cossacks were slashing with sabres at each other's ears while Germans parked their bikes and picked the tsar's kids off big horses with carbines, clay pigeons.

In a drunken flight the Russians stumbled out of World War I and the Germans settled down to sleep and Strauss polkas. Beyond Pinsk lay the Pripet Marshes, mud.

Nothing to eat. No trade. The Jews of Pinsk lived by commerce. An old shoe leather or a tuft of grass was served up. Family fights over a single potato.

Even a rabbi as distinguished as Israel Lehovitch, a rabbi whose family went back to Maimonides, a notable among us, even he felt the pinch. His cheek was hollow where it had grasped him. The flesh fell away from the bone. His daughter Yehoodiss grew up pulling on a lean breast, sickly and wailing.

1919! Yehoodiss was six or seven. The Poles marched into Pinsk. Partisans. They came to the house. "Where's the rabbi?"

"Zionists!" they screamed. "Traitors! Yids!" They pulled the gray-haired rabbi out the door, kicking him. They dragged his wife and the little girl after him. Yehoodiss was swept along with the rest to the market place. She watched 36 men, the leaders of our town, backed up against a wall and shot. A warning! For what—no one knew. Of what—not even the Poles were sure. That's where I lost sight of Yehoodiss, screaming and in tears in the marketplace. I wasn't seeing too straight though, because my uncle was slumped against the wall.

Now I have to depend on the records. Between my memory and where they begin—a few years' gap. I have no papers, no reports, nothing, until . . .

Here! An immigration record. September 1, 1925. It seems that Devorah and Yehoodiss Lehovitch, mother and daughter, have just entered the Dominion of Canada.

The next piece of paper follows too fast. For years nothing, then two right in a row. A death certificate. Made for September 2, 1925, in the name of Devorah Lehovitch. Cause of death unknown. Possible infection of the pancreas.

Those dates, one crouching right by the other. A little girl of twelve in a strange land, no one she knows. Men in uniform speaking another language. Taking her mother away. How many things can you take from a child? What did she see? Her father, wine clotting his white beard, the dead mouth open, kicked by peasants blinking with violence. Her mother under a shroud, carried away by strangers. Gone! Where was she? Gone!

Yehoodiss started screaming in the immigration office. She screamed till her eyes swam in blood. Till the pain kicked her unconscious. Not the last time she screamed.

She was an orphan. Too many in Montreal. The Jewish ghetto there stank in them. Two and three families were crowded into one-room sweatshops, trying to make a living, to crawl up out of the slums. What was left over for orphans? Pennies. She was a ward of the Jewish Welfare Board. It wasn't a board of psychiatrists. A girl of thirteen? Put her out in a foster home. Let her work. Was she any better than the rest?

Now we have reports. Thick and fast. From the social workers. Not too sympathetic. "Refuses to cooperate." Another writes, "Hides in the corners." It looks as if Yehoodiss is a pain in the *tochis.*

I've got a dozen of them. The little girl went from one house to another. Shall we tell you about the Kashlivetskys, who first took her in? Not bad people but deficient in tact. The Kashlivetskys take in three or four foster children. Not only do they get an allowance for their food and drink, but if the girls do a bit of sewing, of piecework, in the afternoon, one can make a dollar or two on the deal. Who is this girl crying over her piece of cloth? You can't sew straight with tears in your eyes. Kashlivetsky has a simple remedy. One that always works with his wife. He gives the girl a slap. And when she starts to scream, he gives her another. Of course, when she rolls on the floor and has fits, that's another matter. Who needs such a girl in the house?

Now she's got to be sent somewhere else. That means paperwork. Now she's causing trouble for the Jewish Welfare Board, too. They are losing sympathy with her case. She needs a good spanking.

They send her to live with Polakovitch, a pickle man whose wife and two daughters work all day over cucumbers in the rooms back of his store. This Polakovitch is a man of few words. The first time he sees Yehoodiss crying, he takes her by the nape of the neck and plunges her head into a barrel of brine. Water therapy!

You think she calms down? Well, for a while. She sits and screws the tops on the jars of the pickles without saying a word. For two weeks she doesn't say a word. Polakovitch is satisfied. He'd let her sit that way for the rest of her life. Would that his wife and daughter would take that little girl and her glassy stare as a model. However, when the representative comes from Jewish Welfare to check up, the representative is a bit disturbed. No answer to "How are you?" No answer to "Do you like it here?"

"How long has she been this way?"

Polakovitch shrugs his shoulders.

"How long?" the visitor repeats.

"Two weeks."

"Not a word?"

Polakovitch nods.

The representative from Welfare snaps his fingers in front of the little girl's eyes. She doesn't blink. The representative feels a twinge of conscience. They could leave her here and no one the wiser but . . . it's not right. Better take her back and find another place.

The Welfare Board knows of a home that wants to adopt a young girl. The family is wealthy and perhaps if it is explained that the girl had a hard time, the people will be understanding. So Yehoodiss was sent to live with Mr. and Mrs. Charlipoff. Mr. Charlipoff is in the fur business. The winter is cold in Montreal so Charlipoff the furrier lines his pockets. Mrs. Charlipoff needs more than her mink stole, though, to keep her heart warm. She wants a little girl to make a fuss over.

She makes a big one over Yehoodiss. She buys her dresses, coats, jewelry. She takes her to the movies, restaurants, etc. Yehoodiss begins to speak a few words.

Encouraged by this, Mrs. Charlipoff bears down on Yehoodiss, a locomotive. Between meals she plies the little girl with sweetmeats, candies, cookies. She unloads a double portion on the girl's plate. She stands over the little one, anxious that she shovel it all down. How many caramels, fudge cookies, chocolate cakes, marshmallows and pistachio nuts in an hour? Mrs. Charlipoff tried to cram pounds down Yehoodiss' throat. Then took it to heart, a reflection on her cooking, when the child didn't swallow extra portions during meals. In a week's time Yehoodiss was sick from overeating and they had to bring her to the doctor.

"Don't worry," said Mr. Charlipoff in the waiting room.

"A delicate child," Mrs. Charlipoff said fearfully. "I'm afraid. Too delicate! Too delicate!"

However, Mrs. Charlipoff was persuaded to bring her love down another track. The little girl seems bright. She ought to go to school. Or, since it's been a while, the best thing is to hire a private teacher.

A teacher is brought in. A young woman, recent graduate from college, not too much experience but full of enthusiasm. The child doesn't know English so it is decided to start her on that first.

In the overstuffed parlor of the Charlipoffs the lessons are begun. Mrs. Charlipoff, anxious for Yehoodiss, sits in. She wants more than anything for the child to succeed. The little girl hesitates for a second, Mrs. C. jumps in with the answer. The teacher has no sooner opened her mouth to ask Yehoodiss a question than Mrs. Charlipoff leaps ahead to cry, "How come you don't know?"

In the middle of the little girl's wavering replies, Mrs. C. exclaims, "Ask her something else!" The mother-to-be shakes in her plump chair with nervousness for her baby's progress. "Is she slow? Is she slow?" Mrs. Charlipoff shouts in despair after 15 minutes.

The teacher begins to get nervous, too. She mixes up questions and answers, confusing herself and Mrs. Charlipoff. As for Yehoodiss? She stares at her new mother and the teacher.

It was decided, quickly, English wasn't that important. The child would pick up English around the house. Or out in the street with other children. Though Mrs. Charlipoff didn't let Yehoodiss out of her sight, let alone out of the house. She bent over the girl, petting her, smoothing her hair, whispering, "Do you love me? Do you love me?"

Canada was bilingual. And French was the language not only of the Province of Quebec but of the civilized world. A young lady ought to know French. Let the girl learn what would be considered an accomplishment.

Only one problem! The teacher's French wasn't that good. In fact, though she would admit it to no one, it consisted of a few catch phrases, "*Au revoir! Aujourd' hui! Je vous aime.*"

Mrs. Charlipoff's French was on the same level. The teacher went home each night and tried to memorize a little for the next day's lecture—Mrs. Charlipoff did not.

They tripped over one another, stumbling on every other word. Mrs. Charlipoff cried with frustration. Rising in her chair, she called out, "The little one's a dummy! A dummy!"

Yehoodiss almost stopped talking again. She was afraid to open her mouth before the teacher. Yet the sound of despair that Mrs. Charlipoff made when she didn't answer—the little girl would say anything.

Meals. "Tell Daddy what you learned!" Mrs. Charlipoff would shriek, then burst into tears as Yehoodiss started to explain.

"Nothing! Nothing!! She can't remember nothing!!!" wailed Mrs. Charlipoff as Yehoodiss was trying to say, "*Aujourd'hui.*"

Finally Mr. Charlipoff intervened. He told his wife to be quiet. Maybe the child had talent in other directions. What did it matter if she didn't speak a perfect French?

Mrs. Charlipoff took hope. Perhaps the little one was an *artiste.* Mrs. Charlipoff had always wanted to be a dancer. Maybe Yehoodiss was a ballerina. She enrolled the girl in a ballet class.

They go off to the first session. Mrs. Charlipoff is trembling.

No sooner do the little girls line up in their tights and begin to try the *plee-ay* under the teacher's direction, Mrs. Charlipoff shouts, "How's she doing? Third from the left, how's she doing?"

The teacher, who has been helping another child, at the other end of the line, looks up and, not wanting to seem indifferent to the ward of the parent, says over her shoulder, "Straighten your left leg a bit."

"Your left leg! Your left leg!" Mrs. Charlipoff calls out in a voice that almost shatters the mirrors. Yehoodiss begins to tremble at the bar. Every limb of her body starts and she can hardly go through the movements or hold onto the brass rail.

Mrs. Charlipoff is trembling, too, biting her lip, pulling at her hair, her breast heaving. The child she wanted to adopt—a spastic!

In each class that follows, Yehoodiss gets worse. Mrs. Charlipoff can barely face the little girl at the table. Yehoodiss can't hold on to plates, cups or saucers. She drops them in nervousness.

Mrs. Charlipoff drops things, too. "She makes me shake!" cries Mrs. C. as the Wedgwood creamer drops out of her hand and shatters on the hardwood squares of the dining-room floor. "She makes me shake! Shake!" And Mrs. Charlipoff starts to scream and cry. She throws down her head on the ringing table.

"I'm sorry . . . says Yehoodiss in faltering English, ". . . *je vous ai*—" trying to put her trembling hand on Mrs. Charlipoff's head that rocks back and forth, nose in a plate of *kishka.*

"Get away! Get away!" shouts Mrs. Charlipoff, then raising a dripping head to her husband, cries, "She doesn't love me! She doesn't love me!"

"I'm sorry," said Mr. Charlipoff to the Welfare Board. "A nice girl. Only a little nervous. Her hand shakes. Not right for us." He brought her back to them in a new fur coat. A gift from him, thick Persian lamb with an ermine collar. Yehoodiss shivered in it. Mr. Charlipoff felt bad. He kissed the girl goodbye.

Montreal was cold. Yehoodiss was shuttled from one place to another. How many people want to board a girl with trembling hands? She dropped things all over their houses. And she hardly said a word. Some of the places she went swore to the Jewish Welfare Board that they had been stuck with a mute. "Put her in a hospital!"

The social workers began to grow peevish. Their reports are before me, larded with adjectives. "Stupid." "Retarded." "Antisocial . . ."

Yehoodiss suckled the sour milk of our charity. She became a dumb beast. Why should she speak? Did she have a good taste in her mouth?

After a few years they gave up trying to board or find a foster home for her. Welfare looked around for some place that Yehoodiss could work. With those hands there were few jobs she could hold on to. Again she traveled from one to another. At last the synagogues were approached. In the house of the president of one Yehoodiss was placed as a maid. He did it as a favor. She made beds, dusted, swept, and was allowed to lay the silverware on the table.

The president, Meyer Mandelbaum, was a gregarious man. He and his wife paid little attention to the girl who slept in their attic and went silently about her tasks. They had two daughters to marry off and were busy inviting young men home to meet their beauties. For eight years they brought home for dinner every available Jewish bachelor in Montreal and any eligible one that was passing through. What was the trouble? There were plenty of candidates in the ranks of the ignorant. The Mandelbaums wanted a scholar. These were at a premium in Montreal. Also Meyer, in addition to his line of woolens, was known to make money as a loan shark. Once known, polite excuses were in order. Every time they opened up the paper and saw a smart Jewish boy marrying, the Mandelbaums groaned. They knew him. It was a personal rejection. And as eight years became nine and nine turned to ten, Meyer stalked the synagogues of Montreal, shaking his head, looking for new faces.

So it was, of course, known to Meyer and his wife when a young rabbi, unmarried, came for a day from the United States to visit his Aunt Rochelle. The Mandelbaums broke down the door of Rochelle's apartment in their haste to grab the young man and snatch him off for supper.

His protests were naught. They bore him off, trying to wave goodbye to Aunt Rochelle.

The youthful rabbi found himself deposited at the Mandelbaums' table, a dazzling expanse of white linen, sparkling on sterling silver, glinting in the gold rims of china. One dish after another was lifted under his nose for a sniff of approbation and his attention directed again and again across the table to the Mandelbaum beauties, *their* excellences, too. Did he favor one or the other? The anxious gaze of the parents flitted back and forth.

As the dishes were cleared, the room became tense with anticipation. The maid's hands began to tremble. Bending over the rabbi's place she fell between him and the fiery gaze of Mrs. Mandelbaum. Scalded, she shook and dropped the silverware into the rabbi's lap.

"What a girl! What a girl!" shrieked Meyer Mandelbaum. "A *klutz!* Get her out! Get her out!"

Tears welled in Yehoodiss' eyes. She began to hiccup hysterically.

"No, no!" cried Rabbi Lux, jumping up from his seat. "It's nothing, please."

Yehoodiss shook so violently she seemed on the verge of a fit. The rabbi patted her back to try to calm her. He put his arm around her shoulder to still the shudders of her body. "It didn't hurt anything. It's good luck, a little accident."

Seeing the rabbi's arm around the maid, Meyer was having paroxysms of his own. Lux turned to him, "Good luck! Good luck!"

And the rabbi smiled so brightly that all the silver, tablecloth and gold rim seemed dim. He smiled for the first time that evening and with such fullness that

Meyer decided maybe it was good luck. If Meyer could get the wedding goblet under the heel of Rabbi Lux, he was willing to break every plate on the table. President Mandelbaum picked up the glass of wine under his nose and toasted the accident, "Good luck!"

Everyone at the table smiled, even Mrs. Mandelbaum.

"Let me say a few words to her," said Rabbi Lux and without heeding the immediate chorus of "She'll be all right. . . . She gets over it in a minute. . . . It happens all the time," he caught the fluttering hand of Yehoodiss between his two soft palms and gently led the young woman into the kitchen.

By the warm stove he let go of her hand. She began to breathe so hard, he feared her breast would shatter. He caught up her hand again. "It was nothing. Why do you shake so?"

Yehoodiss said nothing. Only the resonant sweetness of the rabbi calmed her. She shivered less violently. She tried to speak to his question but the words caught in her throat. She began to cough.

"What is your name?" A syrup of honey, the rabbi's tone smoothed the cords of her voice.

She whispered, hoarse and timid, "Ye . . . hoo . . . diss."

"Yehoodiss what?"

"Yehoo . . . diss . . . Le . . . hov . . . itch"

Rabbi Lux let go of the young woman. She looked up at him, terrified. He stared at her. The black, intense eyes, the high break of her nose, the strong yet full curve of her lips?

"Lehovitch of Pinsk?" he asked in wonder. "Are you the daughter of Rabbi Lehovitch of Pinsk?"

Yehoodiss burst into bitter tears. She began to weep. The Rabbi caught her up in his arms. She flooded his chest with waves of her sorrow. "*Vey ist mir!*" he exclaimed, hugging her. "*Vey ist mir!*"

Meyer was banging on the kitchen door. "*Vas toutsta!* What's up! What's up! *Nu? Nu?*"

"Wait! Wait!" cried the Rabbi.

But the Mandelbaums couldn't—all four came stampeding through the door. "What's going on?" shouted Meyer, seeing Yehoodiss in the young Rabbi's arms.

Lux hugged the maid to him. "You know who you have here? You know who?"

"What have we got here! What?" shouted Meyer.

"A Lehovitch of Pinsk! A Lehovitch!"

The Mandelbaum family was speechless. Meyer could tell the genealogy of every loan and note of hand in Montreal, but he was shaky on the sages of Israel.

"A Davidic line!" cried Rabbi Lux. "And from Maimonides!" He kissed the trembling girl on her cheek and looked up beaming at the wonder-struck Mandelbaums. "And cousins to the Luxes. She's my cousin."

Yes, it was true. Yehoodiss was a fifth or sixth to the rabbi. The next morning Aunt Rochelle came to take the young woman away. Rabbi Lux came, too. He extended his vacation two weeks and spent every day talking to his cousin.

You know Rabbi Lux. He could lure a tale of pain out of a stone. The young woman unburdened herself to him. She who was previously mute began to talk, slowly at first, in crippled sentences, words and phrases wired awkwardly to one another that relapsed into silence every other moment, that had to be picked up by the rabbi and encouraged to try a few steps again. Then inch by inch, leaning on the crutches of his smiles, the sentences faltered forth for a minute or two. Finally, supported on the soft cane of his affectionate arm when they went walking, Yehoodiss and her vocal cords were on the way to a full recovery. In no time she went from minutes to hours. When the rabbi had to leave Montreal, they continued her therapy on the telephone. At the end of two months Aunt Rochelle sent her nephew a copy of the two-hundred-dollar bill she had just paid. Yehoodiss had run it up on the Canadian end of the conversation. Underneath the total Aunt Rochelle wrote in red ink—"Get Married!"

Back to the telephone in the Lux apartment. Yehoodiss, as we see, had an affinity.

CHAPTER FIVE

A CONVERSATION

THE TELEPHONE!

Ah yes, the telephone. We began with that telephone. The rabbi was kneeling before it.

Yet to the rabbi's credit, it must be admitted, that somehow he foresaw such a scene. Who knows how? But he felt the presence of something evil fluttering in the air when Yehoodiss first broached the subject of a telephone.

He objected immediately. As soon as she suggested it, he shook his head. Rabbi Lux, who usually took a day or two to make a decision, immediately shook his head. For the first time in their marriage he questioned Yehoodiss—"Do we need it?"

"Yes!"

"What for?"

"To talk!"

"We don't talk?"

"Not enough!"

"We'll talk more."

This was the first round. Yehoodiss was stopped in this one because she was unprepared for opposition. The rabbi had taken her by surprise. The breath was knocked out of her for a few hours.

Later, in bed, she grabbed the rabbi and came on fighting. Right up to his ear Yehoodiss crawled and whispered loudly, "A telephone!"

It was as if someone had hiccuped in Lux's ear. Startled, he turned over and faced his wife. "A telephone?" he asked, blinking.

"A telephone!" she answered.

"We haven't done without one?"

"No more!"

The rabbi rubbed the sleep out of his eyes, awoke to the determination in his wife's voice. He sat up and asked innocently, "Who else has one?"

"Everyone in Dorchester," snapped Yehoodiss, impatient at evasion.

"In the morning we'll discuss it," said Rabbi Lux. Turning back over, he pretended to go to sleep.

Facing the angry face of his wife across the breakfast table, Rabbi Lux became sick. Already the telephone had brought deceit, evasion into his life. Already, without its even being there. "A telephone!" barked Yehoodiss.

"What if it rings on the Sabbath?" asked Rabbi Lux reasonably.

Yehoodiss smiled at him. "We'll take it off the hook on Shabbes." A concession. She had made him a concession. Rabbi Lux smiled back at her.

"We'll talk more," he said.

Yehoodiss blushed a dark red in her face. Her voice trembled. "You want I should talk to the wall? I should talk to the linoleum when you're away? Who should I talk to?"

"Maybe in the sisterhood, you could . . ." But Rabbi Lux never finished his sentence. Such a look came over his wife's face. He rushed to the sink and got a glass of water. He sprinkled her face. He smoothed her hair. What could he do? Was it worth it to destroy a life for his peace of mind? Some force wanted entrance to his house. A man can resist evil only so far. To resist further was an act of pride. Or so it seemed to Rabbi Lux. He stroked his wife's hair and whispered, "It's all right, it's all right. We'll put it in. Right away. It's all right. It's all right."

And so the little black line, almost invisible, crept into the house of Rabbi Lux, crept in through a tiny hole in the wall. It crept in and gained the ear of Rabbi Lux.

CHAPTER SIX

A CONSOLATION

SOMETIME before this a terrible thing had happened. "Terrible," I mean it. Somewhere, far away, somebody started something. The people who make it their business to know what goes on in the middle of nowhere heard about it.

These people don't know what is going on here in Dorchester. But way over there they knew exactly what was happening. Some *nudnicks*, from the north of some line, went and invaded some *nudnicks* on the south of it. And it seems that we in Dorchester were committed to help the *nudnicks* on the south side.

Who was the first from Dorchester to enlist? Mrs. Blatz's little Harvey. Little Harvey Blatz with the first blush of pimples on his face, whose mother used to call for him at Roxbury Memorial High School every afternoon and chaperone him home on the trolley; little Harvey ran away and enlisted. He joined the Marines.

Mrs. Blatz went crazy. Her sixteen-year-old Harvey! War is not a game for kids.

She called up her neighbors to get him back. She called up the lawyers in Dorchester to get him back. She would have called up Rabbi Lux, but at that time he had no phone. The other rabbis in the community had to bear his burden.

Then she began to write. She wrote to her congressman. He wrote back immediately.

Dear Mrs. Blatz,

We all know that the boy will do proud by us here in the district. May the luck of the Irish be with Harvey, God love him!

Sincerely,

Michael Feeney Flanagan

HON. MICHAEL FEENEY FLANAGAN

P.S. Don't you and the rest of the Jews in Dorchester forget to come out and give me a vote this November.

So then Mrs. Blatz wrote to her senator. She wrote to the Secretary of the Army, the Navy, the Air Force. She wrote to the Secretary of Defense. She wrote to the President. She wrote to the President's wife. By this time her letters were incoherent. Too bad! And does Bess Truman understand Yiddish? Maybe if she did, Mrs. Blatz's letter would not have gone unanswered.

Then someone told her. "Don't say nothing." A neighbor told her, "They find out he's sixteen—they lock him up. For good!"

Mrs. Blatz wasn't sure that wasn't such a bad idea. If Harvey was safely locked up, she could go and keep an eye on him. But the neighbor convinced her it was a bad idea. "It's not a regular prison," whispers the neighbor. "They feed them green paint. They turn yellow. It's a prison that's a paint factory. The fumes! In six months they turn yellow and die. Keep your mouth shut, for Harvey's sake, believe me."

This frightened Mrs. Blatz out of general hysteria. She turned to the specific problem of locating Harvey.

Now she found people to help her. The Red Cross turned up dozens of Harvey Blatzes for her, all over the world, in Okinawa, Tokyo, Singapore, Germany, Spain, Iceland. A pen pal she became. She corresponded with Harvey Blatzes from full colonel to airman basic. None of them was hers. Mrs. Blatz was about to make calls again, about to call up the generals in the world and ask if maybe they had seen her Harvey when . . .

She gets a postcard from her Harvey. Her Harvey! From the first line she hears the genuine ring of her Harvey:

Ma! Guess what? I'm here.

HARVEY

Mrs. Blatz looks at the postmark—Pusan, Korea. And she almost has a heart attack.

But other cards come in after this one. Medals, too! Her Harvey is becoming a hero. Harvey starts sending her gifts. Cigarettes, candy bars, pictures of himself, a captured North Korean helmet, a bayonet with "To Mom" scratched on it. Mrs. Blatz stacked them up in a corner of his room, waiting for Harvey's return.

And what happens? Suddenly, as if Fate had snapped her fingers, nothing arrives one morning. Every day, since the first postcard, something has come in the mail from Harvey. Either a postcard, or a small package, or a notice to pick up a large one at the local post office. For the first time in six months nothing comes. Right away Mrs. Blatz gets worried. She calls up the post office. Nothing there. Then she stops. She sits down in a chair in Harvey's room, one with a slipcover she made herself, and she is holding on to Harvey's last piece of mail. She picked it out of the pile where she had wedged it in neatly the day before. It is a defective grenade. A souvenir on which Harvey scribbled in red "Ma!"

Mrs. Blatz clutches the grenade in her hand and doesn't make a sound. She squeezes it as tight as she can. But she doesn't say nothing.

For a week she sits this way. The mailman doesn't put anything in her box and she doesn't move. The neighbors don't dare to move her. They bring her a little chicken soup and spoon it to her. And they don't stick around to chat. Grenades? Even a little soup could make one go off.

Finally, after a week sitting alone, clutching the grenade, a letter. She hears the postman drop it in the box. It doesn't sound like a letter from Harvey. Harvey is strictly postcards or packages. But Mrs. Blatz gets up and goes to the mailbox. She holds the grenade in one hand. She picks the letter out. It's from the government. It reads:

Dear Mrs. Blatz,

We are truly sorry to inform you that during last week's fighting, your son, Sergeant Harvey Solomon Blatz, disappeared in action and must be presumed either missing or dead.

DEPT. OF DEFENSE
Washington, D.C.

She doesn't drop the grenade. And the postman is still in range. No! She goes straight to the telephone and calls the police.

"Where's Harvey?" Mrs. Blatz asks grimly into the receiver as soon as she hears the officer at the desk pick up his phone.

"Now, who is that, ma'am?" replies a fine Irish brogue.

"Mine Harvey? *Nu?* Where!" asks Mrs. Blatz, biting into her lips furiously as she speaks.

"Harvey who?" asks the genial deep voice at the other end.

"Harvey Blat*zz!*" says Mrs. Blatz, her teeth snapping together in the tzzz.

"Well, where did you see little Harvey last—Mother?"

"I didn't see him!" hissed Mrs. Blatz through closed teeth.

"Well, he's your son, now, ma'am, isn't he?"

"*Nu?*"

"*Nu,* you mean you be letting him roam the streets and not know where he is? Shame on you, Mrs. Harvey! Why they ought to put the boy in the Army and straighten him out. How old is he?"

"He's in Kahrea!" shouted Mrs. Blatz into the receiver.

"Korea?" asked the voice, puzzled.

"*Nu!* Right!"

"Well then, you know where he is . . ." bantered the desk sergeant and he laughed into the phone. Someone was pulling his leg.

"He's missing!" cried Mrs. Blatz.

"Well now, how can he be missing if he's safe in Korea?"

"I got a letter. They tell me he's missing."

"A letter?"

And Mrs. Blatz read the letter. She read the postmark. Read the return address. Described the size, even the texture of the paper. The police had never had a more accurate description of a clue to a missing person, and all the sergeant at the desk could think to stammer was "I'm . . . I'm sorry, Mother. I'm afraid your Harvey is dead."

Mrs. Blatz dropped the hand grenade. It bounced down the hallway and through the open door onto the front porch and down the steps into the street. Mrs. Blatz ran after it. Right into the street she ran, clutching the letter.

"Dead . . ." "Dead!" "I'm sorry—dead." The people she went to see told her—dead. Neighbors, lawyers, doctors, clergymen, all had the same interpretation for the letter—dead. It all came out to the same, no matter how they got around to it, a flat—dead.

Mrs. Blatz didn't take this lying down. "What do you mean?" she demanded.

"I'm sorry but it looks . . ." the voice would begin again, patiently. Mrs. Blatz's mouth was opening with wonder.

"Harvey?"

"Harvey?" She choked for air. "What do you mean?" she shouted. "Harvey?" "You crazy?" "Harvey?" She was screaming—"Harvey? Harvey? Harvey?"

Well, people don't mind this once or twice, but when all week Mrs. Blatz is jumping on you shouting louder and louder—"Harvey?" They were beginning to think of the Boston Psychopathic for her. The neighbors had already called up the police to take her away and the grenade too, please. They claimed she was threatening them with a weapon from the window. Who knows? It was in some state that Mrs. Blatz arrived at the door of Rabbi Lux.

Holding the letter, she knocked on the door of his study in the synagogue.

"*Nu?* Come in," the rabbi called pleasantly. Again Mrs. Blatz knocked. The rabbi got up, came to the door, opened it and saw Mrs. Blatz. Crumpled in her hand was a ball of paper. "What's the matter?" asked the rabbi, concerned.

"A letter!" she barked. Then she shouted, "So, what does it say?"

The rabbi looked at Mrs. Blatz. A big pimple bristling with hairs stood out right over her upper lip—it was swollen and pink from biting on. The bags were unusually dark under her eyes. They looked like thunderclouds, puffed out with the rest of her expression, ready to burst. The rabbi knew Mrs. Blatz. He had personally supervised her son's Bar Mitzvah, a difficult task which had entailed countless interviews with Harvey's anxious mother. He had seen her disturbed, but never like this. Shaking so that she could hardly stand.

"Come in, come," said the rabbi. "We'll read it. We'll see what's in it. We'll find out what it says. Come in, Mrs. Blatz," he urged tenderly. And taking the trembling mother by the arm, Rabbi Lux ushered her to a plump and comfortable chair in the study, settling her among the cushions. Going behind his desk, he sat and read the letter.

The door of the study had been shut several minutes before Rabbi Lux looked up to the intent and awful stare of Mrs. Blatz's terrified, querulous face.

"Well," said the rabbi, slowly, "it looks like Harvey is missing."

"Missing?"

"Missing!"

"Where?"

"I'm not sure. Korea, I think. But probably they're already looking for him."

"How did they go and lose him?" asked Mrs. Blatz,

the tears beginning to trickle down her wrinkled cheeks, the hairs of her pimple drooping.

"I remember," said Rabbi Lux, gently, "when you would come and tell me how he got lost playing on Lorne Street—your own street. And later you found him in a neighbor's coal bin. So? It could happen in Korea."

"It could happen. It could happen," wailed Mrs. Blatz. She had a possibility now to cry over. She could understand that Harvey might be lost. Tears welled in her eyes till her face was splotched and red. She rocked back and forth, moaning, "Oy! Oy!"

Rabbi Lux leaned back in his chair as Mrs. Blatz cried. He stroked the black leather nubble of his psalm book's cover. His stomach didn't feel good. Yet he sensed it was better to let the woman cry. He had seen grief before. It was good if a little of it could spend itself in tears. *Nu!* Now and then he even encouraged her himself, with a faint "oy." Like a skilled analyst who encourages his patients to wander in their thoughts, Rabbi Lux encouraged Mrs. Blatz to weep. Weep, oh ye daughters of Zion. Weep. Weep, oh Jerusalem.

Rabbi Lux was wandering himself, when he realized that the poor woman before him was beginning to come back to herself. She had stopped rocking and begun to sigh heavily, between her fits of tears. Rabbi Lux leaned forward and asked, "Mrs. Blatz?"

"*Nu?*"

"What can we say?" asked the rabbi softly. "A terrible thing. Harvey is missing. You're right. Anything could happen. What do we do in such a case? What do the rabbis say to guide us?"

Here the rabbi paused and thought for a second. "You know," he began, "it reminds me of Abraham and Isaac. Harvey is lost. So was Isaac! All the way to the mountain, don't you think Abraham thought he was lost? And he had to hold a knife to his own child's throat. . . ."

"He sent me a bayonet!" cried Mrs. Blatz. And she began to weep again, coughing hysterically.

The rabbi waited until she had calmed down. He had picked the wrong parable.

He began again, cautiously. A whisper in the study—"Mrs. Blatz?" It echoed across the room and along the shelves of tattered prayer books. "Mrs. Blatz, can I say something?"

The bereaved mother tried to control her trembling. She rasped, "So say something."

"Mrs. Blatz," began Rabbi Lux, softly and sadly. "Who knows what to say? How can you be comforted? The Talmud tells us of a great scholar who lost his son. The rabbi's friends came to comfort him. And he ran away. A great scholar, yet he ran away. He was afraid his friends would comfort him. And when they caught up with him, did they comfort him? They said the wrong thing and increased his grief. So what can I say to you? I'm a rabbi, not a prophet. But don't take it so hard. Children come back. We were talking about Isaac. You know, Mrs. Blatz, Isaac lived! Believe me. He had a son, Jacob."

Rabbi Lux leaned forward. "Isaac lived. And he had a son, Jacob. A good fellow, maybe you heard of him? He had the same name as your late husband—Jacob."

Mrs. Blatz shook her head. She hadn't heard of the other Jacob. But she wiped some of the tears out of her eyes. "What about this Jacob?" she asked hoarsely.

"God blessed Jacob with a son. Not just one son. But one son especially—Joseph. Just like you, this son Jacob loved with all his heart. An apple this little Yussel was to him. Jacob was crazy about him."

"Crazy?" said Mrs. Blatz, looking at the Rabbi. "He was crazy, I'm crazy."

"You're not crazy," said Rabbi Lux, interrupting her, his voice rising. "About children everyone is crazy. You have to be, believe me. Jacob was crazy about Joseph. His heart ached with love just to see him. Jacob always had his eye on him. Nothing was too good for Yusselle. He ran out to get him a coat. A coat of many colors he got him. In those days it was something, a coat of many colors. The best of everything for Yussel. Just like you ran to do the best for Harvey. And if that's crazy, it's all right!"

"What happened?" asked Mrs. Blatz, beginning to get anxious about this Yussel.

"*Vey,*" sighed Rabbi Lux. "One day Jacob let Joseph out of his sight. A growing boy, you can't lock him up. And the next minute, before Jacob knew what was happening, they bring back the coat of many colors. Right away Jacob recognizes it. A coat like that you don't see every day. But his heart faints as he looks at it. Blood all over it. And the cloth is in shreds. It's a rag. What happened? A beast of the field, a lion or a wolf, something terrible, went and ate Yussel. Oy! Jacob is sick. He starts to cry. He weeps. He tears his garments. He heaps ashes on his head. He sits in his tent, moaning and sick to his stomach. Jacob! Poor Jacob!"

Rabbi Lux swayed in his chair, a hand on his stomach. "He was sick as a dog. I know. Believe me."

Mrs. Blatz shook her head. She knew, she knew.

Rabbi Lux continued. "All day he sits in the tent weeping. Who can comfort Jacob? He can't keep his food down. He's upset. With the tears in his eyes he can't see anything. All he can smell are the ashes. He rubbed them in his nostrils. This Jacob was a sufferer, just like you, Mrs. Blatz. He looks for misery. He calls up memories of Yussel, his little one, just to get sick over them. He weeps over the time he pinched the baby's cheek, the time Yussel said his first word. Everything he can remember about the boy, he unrolls it and cries over it. Misery—Jacob knows misery. The acid in his system makes him happy. He enjoys his ill health. As long as he's sick, it's all right."

"But how long can you be miserable? Even Jacob. One day he has to look at his hands, wet and dirty with ashes. He slaps his cheek. He shakes his torn clothes. For the first time Jacob realizes he is a little hungry.

"It happens, Mrs. Blatz. Let it happen to you. You got to live. Would Harvey want you to hate yourself? It's a dishonor to the dead. Take a breath of fresh air. Go to the G & G—have a *nosh.* It's human. Don't hate yourself. For Harvey's sake, let yourself live.

"Mrs. Blatz," said Rabbi Lux, taking his hand off his stomach. "Isaac lived! And Yussel lived, too. All that time Jacob was weeping, Yussel was alive. Jacob swore —he'll go down to his grave in mourning. But God smiles. Why? God knows Joseph is alive. Not just alive. Mrs. Blatz, do you know where they find Yussel? Can you guess?"

"Korea . . ." said Mrs. Blatz.

"Almost as far," "*Eretz Mitzraim.* Yussel is alive in Egypt. He's a bigger man than the Pharaoh. It's a wonderful thing. For thirty years Jacob has been weeping over Yussel and now he finds him. And he's not a little boy anymore. He's an adult. He's got a beard, children. . . . He's running Egypt. . . . He's a success. Who expected it? Jacob hugs him. Jacob weeps, but this time from happiness. Everyone kisses everyone. The whole family is there."

Rabbi Lux, who was leaning over the desk, suddenly sees the clock on the opposite wall. Six-thirty! He's half an hour late for supper. Yehoodiss will have a fit! He rises quickly from his seat. "Excuse me, Mrs. Blatz. I got to go! Take heart. Who knows? Maybe we'll hear from Harvey?"

Fatal last words. As Rabbi Lux rushes from the study, Mrs. Blatz calls hoarsely, "It shouldn't take *thirty years!*"

CHAPTER SEVEN

A COMPLICATION

AS RABBI LUX walked hurriedly home along Blue Hill Avenue, he reviewed his conversation with Mrs. Blatz. Something did not sit well. He had started off badly to begin with. That knife of Abraham's, it had stuck in her heart. And what followed was too glib. A cover-up. He hadn't even convinced himself. He sensed he had said the wrong thing. What does the Talmud say? "If a prayer is fluent in my mouth, I know that it is accepted, and if not, I know that it is rejected."

Rabbi Lux recalled this passage and knew that his advice to Mrs. Blatz had not been fluent in his mouth. He discerned that he hadn't really comforted the woman. He had just quieted her. Rabbi Lux became uneasy in his stomach. He sensed trouble.

Yehoodiss was standing in the hallway when he got home. At the top of the stairs she stood with an alarm clock in her hands. She let it go off in his face, "Ding ding ding ding! Dang dang dang! Dong! Dong . . . !

She looked angrily into his face and then blanched. He was deadly pale, white as whitefish. Yehoodiss threw the alarm clock over the banister and, rushing down the steps, grabbed his arm. "What's the matter?" she cried.

"An Alka-Seltzer," said Rabbi Lux faintly. "I'll be all right. I'm a little late. I couldn't help it."

"Never mind, never mind," said Yehoodiss, supporting her husband through the door of their apartment and into the kitchen. She pushed him into a chair by the table. "Sit down, relax. Better late than never!" she said, standing over him, feeling his cool, moist forehead. "We'll fix an Alka-Seltzer. You'll be better."

So Rabbi Lux had an Alka-Seltzer. It took two or three before he was comfortable. Before his wife, who sat opposite him, across the table, gave up staring at his face for signs of a serious illness.

If only a stomach ache had been the end. How many woes have been thrust down in a stomach? There are even two of them, a big stomach and a little one. Just drop a trouble down into the soft, damp stomach lining. Coat it with a glass of milk. Soothe it with a little Alka-Seltzer. And let it slumber. Half the time when it wakes up, the need for it is gone and you can dispose of anything left, at your ease.

It's so nice and dark down there. A trouble can curl up and sleep forever.

So Rabbi Lux wished that this trouble would join a few others in his tummy and take a long nap. Maybe it would never wake up. What could he do about it? Nothing! He couldn't even talk with anyone about it. Rabbi Lux was a discreet man. He didn't talk about the troubles he heard. Now an indiscreet one like myself doesn't have this difficulty. I have plenty of safety valves. If I hear of a trouble and it is too big for me to forget, I don't swallow it. I run to tell someone else about it. Not just one person, either. I run to ten, 50. . . . The bigger the trouble, the more friends I share it out to. The more who hear about it, the more that are worrying about it. That's my philosophy, it saves me a lot of worry.

Rabbi Lux couldn't do this. How would it look, the most respectable rabbi in the community running around telling everyone's secrets to everyone else? Not that it doesn't happen. Rabbis are storytellers. Look at the Talmud. It's bursting with gossip, names and all. But Rabbi Lux wouldn't say anything. He couldn't even tell his wife. And this was an additional worry.

Because she didn't like this.

Yehoodiss knew that Rabbi Lux was keeping things from her. She knew they were none of her business. But she didn't like the idea of not knowing what was going on in the rabbi's mind. Especially when she saw that these things disturbed him. That they made him come home late. That they distracted his attention from her. Yehoodiss wanted to know what was going on. The Rabbi wouldn't tell her.

It aggravated her. Yehoodiss loved secrets. They were like sweetmeats to her. She was already a central intelligence agency in Dorchester. What she wouldn't have given for a little firsthand from the rabbi. She sat every night with a banquet of information and couldn't get a scrap.

Yes Yehoodis hungered. Not just for information. She hungered for the rabbi, his soul, every bit of him. It wasn't enough that she grasped his plump white body at night in the bed. It wasn't enough that she squeezed him between her heavy thighs and pressed him into her big breasts.

She was jealous of these secrets, these stories that couldn't be told. She watched her kindly but reticent husband out of narrowed eyes and tried to pump him for intelligence. But even in the throes of passion, the rabbi kept a hold on his tongue. Yehoodiss became a tigress, a minx, a squirrel. No matter how many tricks she pulled, the rabbi's mouth remained shut. He sighed and groaned with her, but he said nothing.

And this didn't satisfy Yehoodiss. She wanted to know. She had a right to know. . . .

"What?" the rabbi would ask.

"Whatever!" Yehoodiss replied.

"Whatever what?"

"Whatever's going on in your mind!"

"Nothing," the rabbi answered. "Nothing!"

"Over nothing you fainted on the steps? Over nothing you tried to drink your soup with a fork? Over nothing you have been making sounds all evening? *What's this nothing?*"

"Woe if I speak," cried the rabbi, "and woe if I don't speak." He was in bed by now and he turned over and held his tummy. Yehoodiss knew that a quotation from the Talmud meant the end of the discussion. Disgruntled, she turned over in the bed, the other way, and made angry breathing noises until she fell asleep.

Such a situation is tinder. Yehoodiss' temper was combustible. And the rabbi was holding so much gas in, it was a wonder he didn't explode. They loved each other. They had feelings for each other. That only made it worse. They thought of each other when they should have thought of themselves. In a fire that can be disastrous.

"Ding, ding, ding, ding, ding!"

Rabbi Lux sat up in his bed with a start.

"Ding, ding, ding, ding, ding!"

Five o'clock in the morning. What was it? A fire—whispered Rabbi Lux. Yehoodiss jumped up in a tangle of blankets and bedclothes.

"Ding ding ding ding dong!"

"The telephone," cried Mrs. Lux as she tumbled out of bed onto the cold linoleum in bare feet and began to hop, trailing blankets, toward the kitchen. The telephone at five o'clock in the morning? It must be a catastrophe, thought Rabbi Lux. Yehoodiss had other ideas. It must be some piece of information. She bruised her shin on the bureau going out of the bedroom and stubbed her toes on the frame of kitchen doorway in her haste. At that hour of the morning, it was inevitable that she would slip, collide with the dinette table and, falling, smash, into a chair. A long bleeding cut on her forehead, a black eye, concussion. . . .

"Ding ding ding ding dong!"

Raising herself off the frosty floor, Yehoodiss snatched the receiver from the phone on the wall, put it to her ear.

"Is Harvey there?"

It was Mrs. Blatz. "Wrong number!" Yehoodiss shouted and hung up.

Rabbi Lux tiptoed into the kitchen in his underwear. "What happened?" he asked. "You all right? I heard a crash. *Vey ist mir*! You're bleeding. We better call a doctor." But as Rabbi Lux reached for the receiver:

"Ding ding ding ding dong!"

"The phone," said Rabbi Lux. And then, remembering the call a few minutes ago, he asked, "Who was it?" Yehoodiss rose from the chair where she had collapsed and yanked the receiver off the hook. "Who was it?" she shouted into the phone.

"Rabbi Lux?" came the answer.

"How could it be Rabbi Lux who was it?" cried Yehoodiss, exasperated. "Rabbi Lux is right here!"

"Is Harvey there?" asked the voice.

"What should he be doing here?" replied Mrs. Lux. Turning to her husband, she asked sarcastically, "Is Harvey here?"

"Harvey?" The rabbi repeated the name, bewildered. Then he clapped his hand to his head. "Wait a second. Maybe . . . " The rabbi took the receiver from his wife's hand and spoke into it. "Hello. Is it you, Mrs. Blatz?"

It was Mrs. Blatz. She began to talk so rapidly that the rabbi had a hard time keeping up. "No, Mrs. Blatz. I'm sure. I haven't seen Harvey. No. I haven't heard from him. Yes, as soon as he calls, I'll tell you. Yes, Mrs. Blatz. As soon as I know, believe me. No. No. I won't tell anyone else first. No one else. You'll be the first to know. Believe me, I'll come right to your house. That's all right. It will be a pleasure. A pleasure. No, I don't need anything. It's very kind of you. I won't forget. The first one. Believe me. As soon as I hear. It's all right. Good night. God should take care of you, too, Mrs. Blatz. Good night. That's right. I won't forget. I'll remind myself. Don't worry. That's all right. It's no trouble. That's right. You can still get some sleep. You'll feel better. Good night. Take care too. Good night . . . Good night, I won't. Good night. . . . "

And so on, for ten minutes. When Rabbi Lux finally put down the hook, Yehoodiss was staring at him, twitching her lips. There were a few seconds of silence. Then she blurted out, "So who was it?"

"Mrs. Blatz," said Rabbi Lux. He turned to go back to bed.

"So who is Mrs. Blatz?" snapped Yehoodiss, compressing her lips. Yehoodiss knew that it was Mrs. Blatz. She knew because the rabbi had said the name a dozen times already on the telephone. And she knew from her friends in the sisterhood all about Mrs. Blatz and her troubles. Perhaps Yehoodiss even knew that Mrs. Blatz had been to see the rabbi. The sisterhood at Beth Rachmoniss kept an eye on other things besides cakes in the oven. Yet it would in no way have lessened her irritation. Especially when rabbi Lux answered quickly.

"Business from the *shul*."

"What's the matter?"

"It's private business, I can't say."

"At five o'clock in the morning it's private? At five o'clock in my house, on my phone—it's private business? Private? Public? At five o'clock it's *my* business. What's going on?"

"A poor woman, she lost her son," said Rabbi Lux, appealing to Yehoodiss with open palms to stop the discussion.

"Her son is here?"

"Please, Yehoodiss, forget it."

But Yehoodiss would not forget it. She might have forgotten it. If only Rabbi Lux had opened up his heart and shared some of his troubles. If only he had said to her, "Yehoodiss, the woman is heartbroken. She's half-crazy. The son is lost and . . . he is probably dead somewhere in Korea. But in her condition now, why tell her that? Let her hope, at least for a little while. Her only son. Her one blessing in life. The husband ran away. Her parents are dead and they never spoke to her when they were alive—on account of her husband. *Vey!* All she had was this boy, Harvey. And he runs away, just like the father. If only he had just run away. But he sends a postcard back. He loves his mother. At a distance. He sends her gifts. Knives and hand grenades. Now she loves him twice as much. And then he disappears. And they send a form to her—dead or missing. Let her get used to it. Let her think that he's just missing for a while. Can I tell her that he's dead? Let her avoid it for a while. Yehoodiss, what can I do? You got to have a little compassion. *Rachmoniss* . . . pity. Have a little *rachmoniss* for her."

If only Rabbi Lux had opened to his wife. Aside from some practical results, better digestion, no gas pains, regular movements, who knows what intangible effects it would have had?

But Rabbi Lux was not the man to do that. Rabbi Lux's genius was his composure. It was a gift, however, that could go only one way. Rabbi Lux could give sympathy but he could not take it. A small flaw, a touch, the slightest taint, of pride is in it.

Yet how could Rabbi Lux be proud? His manner was so meek and kindly, almost obsequious. He was charitable, generous, always thinking of others, always trying to understand the world.

Ah yes! He tried to understand the world. Who can understand the world? Did Rabbi Lux ever claim that he could? Well—he never said that he couldn't. What he couldn't understand—he moved away from. He hushed it. He swallowed it. Evil made a stir in his bowels but not in his brains. He sat in the bathroom with a black *pupik*. But his faith was unclouded. What bothered his stomach never troubled his mind. Life was good. He would find the goodness in a person—no matter how ugly his deeds. Through sympathy he would lead the poor fellow back to an understanding of goodness, the goodness in himself and in the world around him. Rabbi Lux already had this understanding. For Rabbi Lux to ask for sympathy would have been to admit that he, the rabbi, did not understand. And this the rabbi could not do. He had a faith in good—so what did he need sympathy for? For his bowels? On that level he would accept it.

Rabbi Lux! Man is a grasshopper. Why didn't you read Isaiah? You think Isaiah was crying for the Jews? He was crying for himself. He knew—God sits on the edge of the universe and has a good laugh. You think good is coming? Not any good, you know. Howl—Rabbi Lux! Howl!

"What's the matter?" cried Yehoodiss, coming up to the rabbi. "What's with Mrs. Blatz?"

Plenty was the matter and not just with Mrs. Blatz. But Rabbi Lux said nothing. He backed out of the kitchen, holding a finger to his mouth, going, "Shhhh . . . shhhh . . . shhhh . . ."

CHAPTER EIGHT

A SANDMAN

THAT "shhhhh" simmered and boiled in Yehoodiss' soul.

"Forget it," the rabbi had cried. But Yehoodiss didn't forget it. And when the phone rang two days later, at seven in the evening—a time when it was unusual for a phone to be ringing, since it was suppertime all over Dorchester—when the phone rang not with a friendly "ding dong" but an insistent and hysterical "ding ding ding ding," Yehoodiss jumped up from her plate of kasha varnitchkas, shouting, "Don't answer!"

"Don't answer?" asked Rabbi Lux. "Maybe it's for you." Before Yehoodiss could stop him, he had gotten up and was answering. "Who? No—he's not here. I'm sorry, Mrs. Blatz. No—I haven't heard yet. . . ."

As Yehoodiss heard the beginning of the conversation she picked up her plate of kasha varnitchkas and threw them on the floor. Then she waited stolidly, as the conversation continued. She sat down at the table and stared at the rabbi, as he tried for ten minutes to disentangle himself from Mrs. Blatz and her recurring questions. She drummed on the table with her fist, louder and louder, until the rabbi was forced to press the receiver like a suction cup to his ear and even shout into the mouthpiece. She was picking the heavy chrome and plastic table up and banging it on the floor when the rabbi finished.

Rabbi Lux sat down at the table. He didn't say anything. Yehoodiss reached over to a big glass salt container. She unscrewed the shiny aluminum top and spilled half a pint over the rabbi's varnitchkas. The rabbi looked at her.

"Eat," she said, looking back.

The rabbi took up his fork and dabbed at a flat yellow noodle on his plate. "It looks a little salty."

Yehoodiss reached over to the crystal sugar shaker, pulled off its plastic nipple and emptied a pint of sugar onto the varnitchkas. The Rabbi looked at his wife. Not a word escaped from his lips. For the remainder of the meal the only sound that could be heard was tsssssp, tsssssp, as the rabbi sipped at his tea, unsweetened.

It went on for two weeks. For two weeks Mrs. Blatz called, the rabbi answered, Yehoodiss dumped supper on the floor. Or dumped such ingredients on their food it was inedible.

Of course, the rabbi began to suffer. Supper was the big meal for the Lux family and he didn't get any. Yehoodiss was treading on the other meals, too. Breakfast at the Lux's used to be an affair—whitefish, rolls and butter, tubs of sweet butter, wedges of cream cheese, loaves of rye and pumpernickel, at least three different preparations of the eggs. I could make out a menu for you—orange juice, pineapple juice, grapefruit sections, half a cantaloupe, French toast, fried matzoh

. . . Yehoodiss would get up an hour early so that the rabbi should come home from synagogue to a full stomach. She set up a dairy bar, a hotel breakfast.

For the last two weeks the Rabbi was afraid to get out of his bed. In a chipped brown dish sat the tailbone of a whitefish, picked clean. Beside the ugly plate stood a glass with a crack running down the side. It was half-filled with cloudy dish water. Rabbi Lux sat down at the table. He took up the glass and moistened his lips with the water. Yehoodiss stared at him. He went through the motions of gargling. "Suck on the bone!" snapped Yehoodiss. "It's good for you!" The rabbi popped the tail of the whitefish into his mouth and began to chew on the fleshless bone. Suddenly he gagged. A sharp edge had caught in his throat. He had to swallow the glass of foul water at his side to wash it down. Sick to his stomach, he got up from the table and went to synagogue, holding the lunchbag Yehoodiss had presented him with.

In the brown paper bag, banana peels, egg shells, coffee grinds, chicken intestines—the garbage bag Yehoodiss had given him. It was wet and dripped all over the rabbi.

Suppers you already know about. You can't eat them off the floor. Not in an Orthodox home. So even Yehoodiss began to suffer. She couldn't bear to eat a big meal by herself. No matter how many delicacies she consumed during the day, her stomach grumbled. She missed the roasts and pudding that were set out for the rabbi's supper. All day she was hungry and yet she couldn't eat a meal. Yehoodiss stuffed herself with sweets, chocolates and sugar-coated almonds.

By the end of the second week the rabbi looked wan and beaten. His head drooped. She could see from across the table that he was breathing slowly, with difficulty. Yet he wasn't giving up. When the phone rang nightly at seven, he got up to answer. He refused to cut off Mrs. Blatz, her connection.

The sweets were cloying on Yehoodiss' tongue. She decided to try a strategem.

She got one of her girl friends to call her up at seven o'clock in the evening. Yehoodiss would be on the phone when Mrs. Blatz called. She would take the initiative.

At 6:59 the phone rang. Yehoodiss jumped up.

"I'll get it," said Rabbi Lux. He picked the phone off the hook and said hello. As Yehoodiss watched his features sadden and slacken, she knew she was beaten.

And she was not beaten just that night. When her friend was to call at 6:45, Mrs. Blatz called at 6:44. At 6:00? Mrs. Blatz called at 5:59. When Yehoodiss got on the phone at 4:00 o'clock, *before the rabbi came home,* gloating, as her husband came through the door and sat down at the table listening to her read recipes out of her cookbook to a friend on the other end, when she finally put down the phone with a satisfied look at eight o'clock and went to get the cheese blintzes off the stove:

"Ding ding ding ding!"

"Hello?" asked Rabbi Lux in agony.

"Hello. Is Harvey . . ."

Three cheese blintzes hit the rabbi in the face. One caught him right in the mouth. He swallowed the cottage cheese and continued, "No . . ."

There was a crash of dishes. The rabbi could barely make himself heard. "No, he's not here. . . ." Yehoodiss had broken the crockery on the supper table. She began to smash the expensive china in the closets of her pantry. On a chair she stood screaming and swept the dishes off the shelves. The noise was deafening. Bits of china and glass flew everywhere.

At the phone Rabbi Lux licked the cottage cheese off his lips. "I'm sorry," he added. "I'm sorry."

Was no one sorry for Rabbi Lux? It was the third week of the fast. He was grateful for that bit of cheese. The only nourishment the rabbi had been getting was a glass of whiskey, a herring shred at *shul.* On an empty stomach it made him giddy. His eyes swayed on the parchment scrolls and he could hardly make out the Hebrew. He knew the passages by heart but he began to mix Isaiah with Esther, the book of Genesis with Exodus.

He was losing his balance. There was a ringing in his ears. At home now, he and Yehoodiss were not speaking. All the cheerful babble of gossip that she used to pour into his ear, silenced. She didn't even scream anymore. When Mrs. Blatz called, Yehoodiss sat and scratched her fingernails on the plastic tabletop. A horrible soundless noise. And afterwards? A dead calm. You could hardly hear her breathe. She was waiting. Whether he rose up or sat down, the rabbi could feel in the house a hysterical quiet. Both of them were waiting . . . waiting. . . . Rabbi Lux began to enter a dream world where the only sound was a telephone. A telephone that rang nightly in the midst of a terrible silence.

Ding ding ding!

Hello?

Hello? Is Harvey there?

Harvey! Harvey! Harvey!

The call was on the line for him at the *shul.* It was waiting for him at home. He lay in bed, waiting for Mrs. Blatz to ring him up again. Half-asleep, half-awake, the rabbi tossed in his covers, waiting for the phone.

Ding ding ding ding!

Deep in sleep the rabbi sat up.

In the darkness before him he saw a telephone. It was sailing toward him, ringing. Loud! It would wake Yehoodiss. The rabbi felt an unaccustomed irritation. He rose in his bed. At this hour?

Unsteadily Rabbi Lux reached forward to take hold of the oncoming receiver but lost his balance and fell. The black cord of the telephone whipped around him. It jerked tight and the armature smashed into his face like a dumbbell. Entangled, painfully, the rabbi was spun about, but instead of hitting the floor, he was jerked upward and whirled like a top out of the bed.

Revolving dizzily, the rabbi gripped onto the telephone. "Hello?" he called. As he fell, one end of the black dumbbell had been jammed into his mouth. The other end pressed into his ear. The plastic armature was pinned by two loops of cord to the rabbi's head. The loops grew tighter and tighter as he spun, forcing the telephone into the rabbi's mouth and ear. It was all he could do to keep from gagging. His ear ached. In his mouth he could hear someone speaking. Low, guttural sounds were coming out of that end of the phone. They tickled his throat.

It was the earpiece in his mouth, realized the rabbi. The mouthpiece must be in his ear. "Hello!" he shouted, hoping that the word would reverberate in his eardrum and make itself heard. The armature tightened against his head. The earpiece was sliding down his throat. A few more turns, the pressure would crack his skull or the black plastic bone would choke him. "Hello!"

The sounds in his throat grew louder. The tickling was almost unbearable. The rabbi closed his mouth over the receiver and tried to force his voice through his ear. There was an enthusiastic response from the earpiece in his mouth. So much so that the rabbi hiccuped violently. The phone flew out of his mouth and then, flying back, banged his lips painfully against his teeth.

"Owww!" Rabbi Lux's mouth stung. His lips were bruised. His head ached. His throat was sore. Despite his self-control, the Rabbi felt hurt. "Why do you pick on me?"

Yet the telephone was no longer to his ear and mouth. An instant before, the rabbi had wobbled to a stop. Now he took a step and discovered that he was on firm ground. The telephone lay at his feet. Someone was still speaking. A faint voice was coming from the earpiece. Cautiously lifting up the armature, he asked, "Hello?"

"Hello. Is Harvey there?"

"Harvey who?" asked the rabbi. He was still a bit stunned from his whirl through space and the smash he had received in the teeth.

"Blatz!" screamed the voice.

"Oh, its you. Excuse me, Mrs. Blatz. How are you?"

"Is Harvey there?" Mrs. Blatz grimly reiterated.

"To tell you the truth," said the rabbi, trying to be polite, "I'm not sure where I am myself. So who knows about Harvey?"

"Find out!" snapped Mrs. Blatz.

The command upset Rabbi Lux. He asked, uneasily, "Is Harvey missing?"

"Find out!"

The rabbi was standing in the midst of darkness, black pitch. He was reluctant to move. "Maybe he'll come home by himself," he suggested. "Wait a while."

"Take a *look!*" Mrs. Blatz spat the words at him through the receiver.

Rabbi Lux's head throbbed. He wanted to put the phone down. Yet he was afraid of offending Mrs. Blatz. He looked about.

Streaks of light began to appear. Far off, the rabbi could make out a jagged line of mountaintops. He called into the phone, "I'm looking."

Through the sky a bleak gray color had spread. The world was mottled in patches of dark and light. The rabbi could see that he was standing in the middle of a broad plain, its surface swampy, disfigured with hillocks and scrub woods. From behind the distant mountains came the echo of bugles. He stared at the far-off heights and made out a faint blurred dot. It was moving. A tiny figure was descending from the hills. It was a soldier, burdened with a large pack. Closer and closer the man came, running.

Rabbi Lux's heart leaped with joy. "Harvey!" he shouted. "Wait a second," he said into the phone. It was yanked out of his hand. The rabbi was too excited to care. It was Harvey. Little Harvey Blatz from the Beth Rachmoniss Hebrew School. There were tears of happiness in the rabbi's eyes. Agitated, he began to run toward the boy. "Harvey! Harvey!"

Harvey Blatz was in an oversized GI uniform. He staggered forward under a bulky canvas knapsack. It was too heavy for him. It was weighing Harvey down.

"You're found!" cried the rabbi, lifting his hands up. Harvey was only a few yards away. Rabbi Lux was ready to fall on his neck with kisses. "You're found!"

Harvey didn't answer. He veered to the side and began to run away from Rabbi Lux. In amazement, the rabbi shouted again, "You're found!" and started to chase after. Harvey had sprinted ahead, but the rabbi could see that he was in difficulty. The ground was becoming increasingly swampy. The Blatz boy was toiling through a thick slough of mud. The heavy pack on his back made him sink deeper into the earth. He struggled to pull his feet, one after the other. The green mud sucked and oozed up to his knees at every step. Mud, mud was everywhere. Harvey thrashed, caught in a quagmire.

Despite his clean rabbinical clothes, the rabbi pushed into the slough after Harvey. The mud oozed in slimy fingers up his trouser legs. Inside his shoes the socks became gritty. And there was a bad smell. As the rabbi churned his way through, he saw that the swamp was really a huge compost heap. Years of garbage had been dumped in the spot. Dead cats decayed among rotting peels of oranges, heaps of coffee grounds, egg shells, bone fragments. All, in a moist state of disintegration, made up a green ooze. It crept like a sluggish stream around the rabbi's calves. He noticed shreds of old prayer shawls and moldy pages from Hebrew books. A stink of putrefying herring rose above all.

The rabbi tried to push faster through the ooze. He was almost up to Harvey. On the edge of a buried sardine can Rabbi Lux cut his ankle.

"Owwww!" The rabbi winced. He tried to lift his throbbing foot out of the acid juices of the muck.

Harvey turned around. Mud, heavy, green, wet like plaster caked Harvey's face, clung to his faint whiskers. A dripping death mask. Harvey began to sink. He was going down uncoffined into the grave.

"What's happening? . . ." A machine gun chattered. Harvey Blatz sank.

The rabbi was down in the mud, too. On his face, upset. He was responsible. Was this a time for Harvey to pull crazy tricks?

The machine gun stopped. Rabbi Lux puckered his lips. Mud trickled out. He wiped his face and started to crawl toward the spot where Harvey had disappeared.

Nu! The rabbi's clothes were filthy. The mother would be angry. This had happened before. Every other week the Blatz boy ran away from home. Rabbi Lux and the police went after him. A familiar situation. The truant Blatz boy hiding behind the ash barrels by the Hebrew school fence. A frantic mother. Rabbi Lux crawling down alleys, searching through the trashcans, begging the child who was hiding under the garbage bags to climb out and come home. Every week! It was enough to make you angry. "Harvey!" shouted the rabbi. And out of the swampy earth rose the pimply face of Harvey Blatz.

Rabbi Lux squinted at the apparition. "You washed your face," he said.

A smile widened in the air. A grin distended the mouth, though the eyes blinked compulsively. A real *shlemiel.* The rabbi was sick. The same stupid look Harvey had in Hebrew school. What could you do? It was true. Why? Why did the other boys always beat him up in the Hebrew school yard? What was the matter with the Blatz boy? Why did he go in his pants at the age of twelve? What made him sit on the bowl in the latrines and keep wiping? He choked up all the toilets and flooded the Hebrew school. Why did he chew on his books? Jonah he swallowed and half of Job. In his desk he started a fire to destroy the texts. Most of the classroom was charred.

Harvey leered at the rabbi. Why did you go bald at the age of thirteen? A head, red and raw. Your face broken out in a blotch, patches of strawberry. Your nose, God made it run, but not grow. A button. A wet squeeze of clay. All right, thought the rabbi. You can't help it. You look a little funny. But must you make faces like a clown?

Harvey ogled Rabbi Lux. A blinking leer from behind

glasses an inch thick. It was that look which drove people mad. It frightened the rabbi. A smile like a bound goat. Harvey leered. Stop it—the rabbi wanted to cry. Stop it.

"Why?" It was Harvey speaking, an inane grin on his face.

"Why what?" Rabbi Lux was confused.

"Why," giggled Harvey, "are they trying to kill me?"

Unnerved, the rabbi was distracted at this moment. Behind him he heard the tramp of marching feet. Harvey and his expression began to fade into the damp air. "Wait, wait," cried the rabbi. But Harvey was gone.

Rabbi Lux turned around. A hundred yards distant he saw a company of civilians and soldiers approaching. They were marching in step, led by a big burly cop in blue uniform. Sergeant's stripes of bright yellow were on the policeman's jacket. Flaming red cheeks and handsome lantern jaw, a lusty brogue when he opened his mouth, marching the troop behind him, shouting commands, "Huyup! Twoup! Thrrreeup! Fourrrup!"

As the cop and his company neared the rabbi, they all burst into song together.

> I got a girl in Savin Hill, honey!
> Honey!
> I got a girl in Savin Hill, babe!
> Babe!
> I got a girl in Savin Hill!
> She won't do it, but her sister will!
> Honey, oh baby, oh!
> Huyup Twoup Threeup Fourup!

"Whose sister?" shouted someone in the ranks. "Yours!" a voice cried. "Up yours!" chimed in a third. Laughter throughout the company.

"Allroight," boomed the Irish policeman, good-naturedly, "now let's cut out the dirrrty remarks. We are approachin' a member of the clerrrgy. Company, halt! One! Two!"

"At ease!" shouted the sergeant. He tipped his cap to Rabbi Lux. "Good morrrnin', Reverend. Can we be of help?"

Rabbi Lux stared up at the beaming face of the tall cop. He looked at the 40 or 50 men behind the policeman, standing at attention in ordered ranks. "Excuse me," he said. "I'm looking for Harvey Blatz from Dorchester."

The sergeant nodded pleasantly. He seemed to be familiar with the situation. "Blatz, eh? A Jewish boy?" he queried.

Rabbi Lux nodded. The Irish cop turned around to his men and called out, "Be on the lookout for a stray *mezuzah,* belongin' to Blatz!" Then, turning back to the rabbi, the cop added in a confidential whisper, "We got some Jewish boys in the company. Don't you worry, Reverend, they'll keep an eye out."

"You think they'll find him?"

"Oh sure, you'd be suproised at what we find. Just the other day we found the left leg of a fellow who'd been missin' for half a year. Won't that family have a happy suproise in the mail! Sure, you never know what we'll turn up. Don't you give up hope now, Reverend. Oi bet we find a nice piece of Harvey to send home to Mother. Why, roight in me back pocket, Oi've got a piece of the McLaughlin boy that'll make his girl in Southie smile." The Irish policeman clapped Rabbi Lux on the back and winked at him.

"Harvey's alive," said Rabbi Lux. "I just spoke with him."

The policeman broke into laughter. "Sure, that's the way, Reverend. Keep it up! You and the boys are doin' a great job. Believe me, Oi see the men and how they pick up when you're around. Why, Oi spoke with Father Flagherty this mornin' and he give the same cock and bull about the McLaughlin boy. Now he knew he'd be talkin' to him in a day or two. And me with the lad's thing in me pocket. But I niver make fun o' the clerrrgy. No, sir. I wished him luck and good mornin'. After all, it's the Father's business. Say hello to him, will you? You may bump into him over there." The cop pointed to the left where thickets and tall grasses obscured the view. "He's tearin' around in there, lookin' for McLaughlin and a few other lads from Southie. Ones he's promised the mothers—be safe and sound."

The sergeant began to chuckle. He took the rabbi by the arm. "Oi, Jesus, Reverend! You should'a seen Monseeneur Marrone, the little wop from Eastie, paradin' about this mornin'. He got here early to look for a whole kaboodle that disappeared last week. 'Mazzoni, Marrachi, Filecki, O'Pizzio,' you'd niver remember the names. And don't he lose his temper when I forget! It's a good thing I don't speak the language, clerrrgy or no. Oh, he's doin' a big business in candles and medals over there in Eastie. Do you know, Reverend," and here the cop bent over to the rabbi's ear. The white fatherly locks of the Irishman shook with merriment. "I don't want to embarrass the Ee-talian boys in the company," he whispered, "but the little guinea tried to sell *me* a rosarrry. A dago rosarrry!" The cop gripped the rabbi's arm and shook with laughter. In the ranks behind him many joined in the mirth. They evidently knew what the joke was about. "Don't stray over to your left," cried the sergeant, pointing to a rocky stretch where a tiny priest in black cassock could be seen wandering. "He'll sell you one, too!" The whole company roared with hilarity.

"He asked me a question," said Rabbi Lux when the laughter subsided.

"Well, what was that?" asked the sergeant, still jocular.

The rabbi smiled timidly. "Why are they trying to kill him?"

The Irishman let go of Rabbi Lux's arm. He stepped back and took a long look at the clergyman. A traffic light, the expression changed. He glared at the rabbi, hard and serious. "What kind of question is that?"

The men in the company had stiffened. They made no noise but stood still as if waiting for an answer. Their faces were sullen.

"Whadda yuh want to ask it for, Lux?" someone piped up from the ranks. The rabbi leaned forward. He recognized the man. It was a Mr. Schwartz, a middle-aged postal clerk who was a member of Beth Rachmoniss.

"You wanna give the Jews a bad name?" another added. The rabbi recognized him, too, a minor ward politician who came occasionally to the synagogue. "We got enough troubles."

"Yeah!" "Right!" "*Nu?*" a number of voices chimed in. There were evidently about half a dozen of the rabbi's congregation in the policeman's company. One of them began to shout at the rabbi: "We always got to ask the questions? Keep your mouth shut! Let the *goyim* do the talking. Stick with your business!"

"Yeah!" "Big mouth." "*Loch in kop.*" "Nuts!" All half-dozen of his co-religionists were cursing at the rabbi.

"All roight! That's enough!" barked the Irish cop. The Jews quieted down. They shifted self-consciously in the ranks.

"Oi'm sorry, Reverend," said the policeman, turning

gravely back to Rabbi Lux. "You'll understand that the boys feel strongly about this, especially bein' in the minority here. There's Cohen in the Sanitation Department and Manowitz whose a recruitin' sergeant, and the others. They're all doin' a grand job. And they're proud of their religion. You can't go around askin' funny questions. For between you and me," and the Irishman again bent to the rabbi's ear, though his tone this time was serious, almost threatening, "they might be soon askin' some funny questions themselves." The cop looked Rabbi Lux right in the eye and added pointedly, "A worrrd to the wise."

"You know," said the policeman. "Oi recall there was a priest, an educated-lookin' fellow, like yourself, around once askin' questions. 'Why?' and that sort of thing, y'know. Well, you'd niver guess what happened to him. For all his books—he went crazy. Loony. Nutty as a fruitcake. They had to put him away in a monastery. He went off his head somethin' terrible. Started screamin' in church. Roight in St. Paul's Cathedral. Spilled wine all over some old lady and tried to choke an old man with the cracker. Got up in front of everybody and urinated on the Bible. The cardinal saw red! Too bad. A bright boy, the lad. Oi was fond of him. Well spoken, y'know. But those questions. That's what they lead to."

"You go home now," said the Irish cop in a gruff but more kindly voice, "and forget all about them. Take a day off. No one'll notice."

The sergeant winked broadly at Rabbi Lux. He swung his billy club out and smacked it into his palm. "Company, ten-hup!" Dress roight, dress! Ten-hup! Forward hah!"

The policeman and his men began to march away.

The cop, however, turned back for an instant to the rabbi, calling out, "If you see Harrrvey, tell him his supper is waitin'."

Someone tapped the rabbi on the shoulder. A tremor of fear ran down his spine. Slowly Rabbi Lux turned. His back was arched. His knees quivered.

In front of him stood Harvey Blatz. The boy's glasses had been knocked off. His helmet was gone. His uniform ripped. The pack was askew on his back. He was still giggling. He ogled the rabbi with weak eyes.

"Harvey, you scared me. Your mother's looking for you."

The Blatz boy continued to grin. His body began to shake. "Why don't you go home, Harvey?" asked Rabbi Lux. "It's not nice here. She's got supper waiting. A hot supper. And she's worried for you. The police are out looking."

Harvey Blatz giggled. He began to titter. "Wwwhy?" he stammered in his silly voice. The rabbi saw that the boy was turning green. In the corners of his eyes tears were trembling. Both of them were frightened.

Harvey turned and started to run away from the Rabbi. "*Nu? Nu?*" cried Rabbi Lux. He was unsteady on his feet but he tried to give chase. "A hot supper!" he shouted.

Harvey fled even faster. Despite the heavy pack on his back, the boy was running across the swampy ground with wide leaps. He yanked his feet out of the spongy soil and scrambled over strands of barbed wire that bloomed from the earth. The rabbi followed, his legs, cut by the sardine can, were caught in the wire and lacerated. Tears in his eyes. His striped rabbinical pants were in shreds.

They came to the bottom of a hill. Rabbi Lux had almost overtaken the boy. "I can't do this all day," he puffed as he came alongside. "I got to go home. A hot supper."

Harvey spun around and opened his mouth wide. It was full of maggots.

Overhead an artillery barrage let loose. The sky exploded, doubled over, exploded again. Rabbi Lux tottered. "No, no . . ." he called. The sky heaved. He fell. The wet ground oozed through his fingers.

Harvey had run to the top of the hill. The rabbi could not get up. A salvo of rockets shook the ground. He gripped the earth. Harvey's mouth—a black hole. Please, please! Terrified, Rabbi Lux felt his bowels turn wormy. Blood seethed through him, bilious. A mounting bombardment tore into the hill. Rabbi Lux started to roll, numb, tumbled down stony flanks. The bottom! He smashed his head on a rock.

"Where's Harvey?"

With an aching head Rabbi Lux looked up. It was Mrs. Blatz. She glared at him.

The rabbi didn't want to answer. He was frightened and sick inside. Tears in his eyes. He giggled.

Mrs. Blatz looked at him. The rabbi was afraid to look back. Where? Why? Don't ask? People were picking on him. Mrs. Blatz stood over him swinging a big black bag. He tried to smile through his tears. Please, he asked silently. Please?

Bending down, Harvey's mother put her hand on the rabbi's neck. He jumped.

"Shhhhhhhh!" she said. She undid the top button of his collar and loosened his tie. Opening his shirt, she pinched his tit.

"Oww!" the rabbi exclaimed. Mrs. Blatz hushed him. "Shhhhh!" she said. "It's good for you." And opening her short, fleshy arms, Mrs. Blatz pulled the rabbi to her and hugged him. "*Bubeleh, bu . . . uuubellleh,*" she crooned.

She sat down on the rock. The rabbi was in her lap. "Oy, *bubeleh,*" she whispered, pinching his cheeks. "Have I got for you . . . for you." Mrs. Blatz roughly squeezed his nose and drew from her black handbag a steaming bowl of soup.

The rabbi looked timidly at the vaporizing broth. There was a sweet smell in the air. A tiny chicken wing floated in the golden fat of the soup. The rabbi looked up tenderly at Mrs. Blatz. Out of her pocket she drew a long silver spoon. She was about to ladle him the first taste when suddenly, on the hill above the rock—

"Mamma!"

It was Harvey Blatz. "Mamma!" he shouted and began to run away. Mrs. Blatz stood up. The rabbi slid out of her lap. "I'm sorry," she said. "I got to go."

"Why?" murmured the rabbi.

"Heschelle!" shouted Mrs. Blatz at her fleeing boy. "Heschelle!" she cried, holding aloft the bowl of steaming chicken soup. "It's hot!" And she began to lumber up the stony hill after him.

Rabbi Lux's head throbbed. It was getting late. Was Harvey alive or dead? Is Mrs. Blatz chasing a ghost? Where are they? The sounds of bugles interrupted the rabbi's thoughts. He heard a prolonged shout from behind the hill.

"Ayyy eeeeeeeeeeehhhhhhhhhh!"

Harvey and Mrs. Blatz appeared on the crest, running.

Over the top of the hill rose a rim of yellow faces. A horde of Chinese boiled over the slope. They were screaming in Yiddish. They had abandoned rifles, hats, jackets, pants, and underwear in their mad scramble.

Laughing hysterically, they bore down on the object of their ferocious charge. The horde of naked yellow men was making an onslaught on Mrs. Blatz and her chicken soup. "*Mein Yiddishah momma,*" they screamed.

Mrs. Blatz ran as fast as her chubby legs could carry her. Harvey had already doubled around and was running past and in front of her, the huge pack bounding on his shoulders. "Throw it away, Mamma, throw it away! . . ." he called back breathlessly to her.

"It's for you, *bubeleh,* for *you!*" Mrs. Blatz shouted in agony. She threw herself down the hill with the tossing broth. The army of Chinese tumbled right after her. Rabbi Lux saw Mrs. Blatz engulfed in a wave of Chinamen. They rolled upon her, licking up the chicken soup. For a second the rabbi saw her body heave above the milling crowd on the hillside, and then with a groan it disappeared into a mass of yellow insects.

"Please! Please!" cried Rabbi Lux. The swarm on the hillside was twittering wildly. "Stop laughing!" It was too much. Everyone was picking on everyone. Mrs. Blatz picked on him. The Chinese picked on Mrs. Blatz. Must the world eat itself up? What sense could you make of it? He was a rabbi, a teacher. Who could understand?

Harvey! He had to find Harvey. It would be all right. A breath of hope filled the rabbi. Supper would wait. Where was he? The rabbi looked in the direction that the boy had run.

A long way off toward the mountains, the rabbi could see a faint dot. It was Harvey. "*Shalowwwwwmmmm!*" shouted Rabbi Lux. The word echoed mournfully off the sides of jagged peaks in the distance. Gathering his coat, in the cold, darkening afternoon, Rabbi Lux began to run after Harvey. A freezing wind filled his black rabbinical coat and ballooned him over the boggy flats. "*Shalom!*" he cried. "*Shalom,* Harvey!"

But Harvey didn't stop. As the rabbi came closer, he

realized that something was goading the boy on. It was the pack on his back. The huge pack was alive and pushing the Blatz boy forward.

Poor Harvey! He ran in circles now, round and round, on the plain. His knees were raw and bloody. He kept falling down. Yet pulling himself up, he staggered on. His heart! Rabbi Lux could hear it pounding in the cold air. Harvey's feet suddenly stuck in the mud. His legs were bare. The flesh was icy.

"Harvey!" he shouted. But the pack now began to move on Harvey's back by itself. A pair of fat legs kicked out of the rotting canvas and in stirrups of grenade belts, jabbed into the boy's sides. It was riding Harvey. The boy tried to jump into the air to free himself but the immense pack only jolted down on him the harder. Gasping, Harvey crawled forward. The pack reared. Harvey was knocked on his stomach. His mouth crammed with dirt.

"Harvey!" screamed the rabbi as the dark shape of the pack rose up. Out of the canvas sack a bulky female figure loomed, bearing her weight down on him. . . . The Rabbi recognized her. He screamed, desperately, "*Yehoodiss!*"

"Yehoodiss!" the rabbi gasped. His wife had rolled on top of him in the bed and he awoke just in time to escape suffocation. He pushed her ponderous bosoms away from his face and panted for air. "Yehoodiss . . . Yehoodiss . . ." Startled, Yehoodiss Lux awoke. She was in tears. "What's the matter?" she asked, drying her face with the nightgown. But the rabbi could only gasp, "Yehoodiss . . . Yehoodiss . . ."

CHAPTER NINE

ANOTHER DIGRESSION

HOW did Rabbi Lux fall into such depths, and further?

A face stares at me, Chaldean lines, beaked nose, lean cheeks, long, pointed beard—one of those faces so ancient that, when reborn among us, we defer. Sensing the old blood line has renewed a lost countenance, that we are in the presence of Abraham, Isaac.

A prince of Ur, no Tartar khan commanded as did the rabbi of Bohost. Before his look the guilty in the congregation lost control of their tongues, began to babble of sins, afflicted themselves severely. Had he allowed, many would have given up goods and wealth to his household, surrendering all for a privilege, the nod of approval.

The rabbi never permitted such things. A Litvak, the rabbi of Bohost lived in the school of Vilna, the scourge of miracle mongers, Elijah the Gaon. The Law, and only the Law, was credited. To make profit out of it was heinous. No one dared to offer him gifts. Despite the size of his congregation, the Bohosta accepted no salary. A tiny inheritance supported necessities.

Those who viewed the rabbi of Bohost and his grip on the congregation, yeshivah, and souls throughout Poland, Lithuania and Russia might think that it was through fear alone. His slanderers among the merry-making or scoffing suggested ignorance, superstition, a people that still shook in terror of a dead code, legalistic formulas of Babylonian academies, thousand years of dust, dry, stiff. Custom mummified in the arid pages of the scholastic tradition. There was no meat here, no drink for the man who had neither time nor brains to master the intricacies. An inaccessible province for a few intellectuals to dwell in. We want to speak to God now! they shouted. Miracles now! And a great rout of Jews followed after seeking it, guzzling, screaming, dancing.

After the noise died down, the scholars still held sway. In the synagogue of the rabbi of Bohost were butchers, porters, peddlers. When the rabbi spoke from his place at the front of the platform, as he threaded among the codes that had puzzled our forefathers in the halls of North Africa, Spain, France, riddles taken up century after century, the Law, the tradition of inquiry, was touched by hands calloused to wood and iron, rested on backs bent by stone, lead. They rocked, obsessed. The rabbi of Bohost could sweep his congregation up in a discussion of clean and unclean, bring them to the tables where Rabbi Joshua, Rabbi Eliezer and Rabbi Akiba sat arguing until they realized that it was no question of an oven being susceptible to defilement:

"It's clean!" declared Rabbi Eliezer. "No," ruled the sages. "That oven is clean. I know it's clean. And to prove it, look out the window at that carob tree."

They looked out the window and the carob was torn up and hurled a hundred yards away. "No proof can be brought from a carob tree," the sages decided. "Know that it's clean!" shouted Eliezer. "Let the stream of water prove it." They looked. "It's flowing backwards," said the rabbis, amazed. They ruled, "A stream has nothing to do with a stove." Eliezer lost his temper. "Let the walls of the schoolhouse fall." And the walls inclined to fall, only Rabbi Joshua said, "When scholars are engaged in a legal dispute, what have you to interfere?" (In honor of Rabbi Joshua they did not fall, in honor of Rabbi Eliezer they remained inclined.) And now, Eliezer in tears cried, "If I'm right, let a voice declare it from Heaven." And a voice rang out, "Why do you fight with Rabbi Eliezer? The Law is with him." Only Rabbi Joshua stood up and said, "You gave us the Torah on Sinai. "That's it. A majority overrules. No voices from Heaven."

Yes, the rabbi of Bohost made it clear that the Almighty was told not to interfere. The porter joined the Holy One as He walked around heaven laughing with joy, "In this hour my sons have defeated me." The cheeks of the peddler glowed as the sages ruled that God was to mind his own business. After Sinai Jews were on their own. Man makes the rules. No miracles. The ruling filled the soul of the butcher, making him reel in the pew.

Some might detect in the discourse of the rabbi of Bohost a strain of heresy, a Judaism older than even the Karaites who refused to accept any laws detailed outside the Bible. A dark, pessimistic philosophy that refused, as did the books of Moses, to discuss an afterlife, would not hold out hope of a resurrection, a sense of life as lonely, alien, being and nothingness. A century early, or centuries too late.

He remained unmarried through his youth. It was at the age of sixty that he gave up his bachelorhood and became betrothed, not to a wealthy widow or the daughter of a prominent rabbinical family but . . .

A bankrupt tapster, an innkeeper from a small coach stop far on the outskirts of Bohost, whose wife died in childbirth, would come to the Lithuanian synagogue at intervals of a year or so, stand at the back without a seat, to hear. He brought his daughter, afraid to leave her behind among the drinkers at his ramshackle house. Rachel was the girl's name. Deposited at the door of the women's gallery, she wriggled and crawled through the packed ladies, under legs, skirts, heavy fur wraps, through the smells of perfume, powder, to the balcony rail to see the glittering procession below, the gold filigree of the inscription above the ark, the cherry and blue of the Torah coverings, the polished wooden knobs frosted with silver bells and tiny crowns, elaborate wedding cakes around which the men in black-banded shawls threw their arms and carried to let the lucky ones on the aisles reach out for a taste, kissing the cloth. Everyone singing led by a short jolly man in a black gown with a silk bowl on his head topped by a velvet puff.

And then, rising from a carved wooden throne, she saw a face so white, gray steel lock curling at the man's forehead, a beard of fine wires, a shining dagger above his chest. Rachel, leaning over the brass rail, could not understand what he said at first. He began to tell a story.

A child's tale . . . it comes down to us. The young student, poor, fearful to push himself forward, his ignorance, desperate to learn, stopping at the door of the schoolhouse, his Hebrew is not perfect, the sentences stammer in his mouth. Already other students have looked at his shame. It has been noticed by the scholars. His clothes are in rags, his shoes awful to look at, the cold comes up through the holes. He feels like a beggar. A hundred times he approaches the schoolhouse, a hundred times turns back. He doesn't have the fee for the porter.

Only, none of the students are there today. Not even the elect whose names we will meet as they grow older, sages in the Law. It is a rare day in this dry, warm country. Snow has fallen. Snow as we know it here. A storm. Flakes are whirling in the streets, drifts piling up against the walls, ice hanging from the eaves. Every puddle is a mirror, drops freeze on the nose and lips. The students are home under as many blankets as they can find. Only the masters are in the schoolhouse, warming themselves over the fire of Torah. The poor student can hear their voices when he approaches the door. And at last, tormented by the bits of commentary he hears, lingering at the portal, he turns, springs toward a trellis and climbs to a skylight on the building's roof.

Why do the rabbis love the story? The young beggar lying on the skylight, listening, lost to the cold drift that is piling over his head.

Is it just a story of zeal? A folktale? There are few such storms in Jerusalem. And as it is passed down, it is embroidered. Perhaps we lose the sense of it in the details. For it is not because the student endured such privation for the sake of learning, it is because he pushed himself forward. Tell your own ending. The burden of ice and snow sent him crashing through the glass. The rabbis noticed a shadow over the discussion. Looking up, they see a stiff, pale form. He comes to their attention!

Perhaps he understood little of the commentary, his grammar is weak, self-taught. He is taken into the midst of the sages, unlettered, because his desire is holy, holy.

At this moment, looking up, the rabbi of Bohost noticed the little girl staring at him, rigid on the rail. The next word shattered in his mouth.

A girl of nine or ten, it was unusual, less so there than here but still, a few years from infancy. The rabbi had seen into those eyes. He bent to the beadle and told him to inquire.

Strange, the tapster was a distant relation, an almost forgotten branch of the rabbi's family. He insisted they stay for the holidays that year and made arrangements with a wealthy family in Bohost. It was during this time that the marriage contract was mentioned. In ten years, with the approval of the bride, they would go under the canopy. In the meantime, the family with whom she was staying agreed to board her.

At seventy the rabbi married. Ice in his beard. Rachel became pregnant, delivering nine months after she left the white silk awning.

Through the tiny pearls of the marriage photograph in the Lux's living room, you can barely see that family resemblance her husband recognized in the crowded synagogue. The eyes, more secret than the rabbi's, escaped the shutter. What transferred to the paper just shadows, a black light dimming the white glow in which it floated. And the high bone, the shelf through the cheek, is smoothed, planed away in the prism of silver drops. Only the suggestion of the full bosom at the bottom and nothing that would allow you to imagine her grace, voice, its perfume.

Wonder that little boy was in love? A mysterious, older playmate, they wandered in a garden of stories, adventures, suprises, shared cakes, games. Often the rabbi joined them. He would get down on his knees and crawl around the room. He laughed at their tricks, sang songs at the table, and became a practical joker. Rachel mothered them both, teasing and scolding at some prank they played, hiding her pots, putting a rock in the oven, pretending to be deaf at table.

You would hardly recognize the stern rabbi. In public the awe in which they held the Bohosta did not diminish when he was blessed with a child. The graduates of his yeshivah had gone out all over the world, some to become great bankers, others to found the state of Israel, a few to follow him in the rabbinate. From Bohost young men went to Berlin, Jerusalem, London, New York. In Bohost, they said, he loves a question. Job was his favorite book. That the answers were grim only elated him. He directed his students into science, politics, finance. Ask, he commanded, ask better ones than me.

The austere hawk that sat in his eye when he lectured or greeted the congregation, flew off as he crossed the threshold of his house. If he was unyielding in the Law, there was nothing he would not do for his wife or little one. Candy in his pocket, a gift, cookies he had wrapped up from a celebration in the synagogue. If the boy wanted to sing, he would come late to services. If his wife looked at him sweetly, he would close the book he read, come over and run fingers through her tresses. Outside the house, a world war raged. The rabbi's family knew little of it. The life inside his rooms was a fairy tale.

The little boy grew up in one. His father embroidered the stark pages of the Torah till the scroll glowed with the thousand colors of rabbinical needlework. Even the snake, that stinking thing that crawled out of the Garden fouling our innocence, its fang of poison sunk into our souls, as commentators wound it round their fingers became a wondrous, ruby-scaled creature, beautiful to behold. Exclaimed Rabbi Simeon ben Manasia, "Alas for the most useful servant that was lost to the world! For had not the serpent been cursed, every Jew would have been given two for his personal use at home; one he would send to the west and the other to the east, to bring thence gems, precious stones, pearls and every desirable thing in the world and no creature ever able to injure them. They could have been employed in the place of camels, asses and mules to provide manure for gardens, orchards. . ."

His mother remembered for him how one-eyed Yaakov could balance a green bottle on his flat nose, twirl a knife in flips and somersaults, make a violin sob or laugh. The same Yaakov who broke green glass on her father's head juggled the knife into his best friend's ribs and, after luring tears to the violin, chased her upstairs with lewd shouts. The mud holes floating spoiled cabbage, filth in the inn yard, became ponds by green meadows, scrawny chickens fat geese. All horses were powerful, princely creatures, not a whisper of the ill-tempered beast that was beaten to death under her window, not the nags who stumbled between wagon poles, sides bleeding from the Master's whip, none of the the world she had cried the dark circles under eyes for.

Did the boy hear the sad note that crept into the throats of fat geese and princely steeds? Or raised upon a blue velvet cushion to the bema, understand the black song as his father, the rabbi, spoke of the grave, evil in man, drew a pessimistic commentary for the congregation that sat deep in misery, the aftermath of the war?

The rabbi stared at Europe in rags, its belly rankling, acid, defeated hopes. His students abroad asked him to move and the questions they raised could not be dismissed. Russia was embarked on a course hostile to inquiry. Germany was confused. Poland beset with problems other countries had solved. For five centuries his ancestors had lived to the east of Germany. For a thousand in Europe. That was a sentimental answer. The Messiah had not arrived. Why tarry for his coming in Bohost?

Others pleaded their dead, relatives, employment. The rabbi could not accept such answers. Something stirred in him, an instinct that had displaced his ancestors from Babylon to Palestine, to Babylon again, Africa, Germany, Poland. The history of his people bore out the Scribe Ezra's warning, from his time on, no more miracles. For the rabbi of Bohost, now with a family to look after, that was a strict admonition.

He accepted the invitation of an American synagogue, packed his books, his few belongings, and, in a final sermon to his flock, advised them to do likewise.

So the Lux family escaped the holocaust. A hole was to open up in Europe and swallow six million. Fat geese, skinny ones alike, all were sucked in. A family of thousands, my son and I, the last of the name. I, who meant to be in the midst of a great table, hundreds of cousins, nephews, nieces, to see me into old age. If the little boy had to look into that hole, he might have had a different point of view.

Only he was not permitted to see even the ditches of that postwar landscape. Breaking his own rule, the rabbi accepted a gift—first-class accommodations. As the train sped across the Continent, he pulled the curtains down on the horror and entertained his boy with conundrums. The child's head was buried in furs, his mother's lap. At each stop the leaders of the Jewish community came to the train with baskets for them, honoring the Bohosta. In their gaunt faces the rabbi read the cost of the offering. He could not refuse. Later he broke off in the middle of jokes and lullabies, could not eat the elaborate dainties, finally, excusing himself, walked down to the third-class carriages to give the food away.

At night he moaned in his seat as the train moved through ruined towns and villages. His tiny son woke, resting on his mother's smooth cheek, and looked with fear at his father's face, for the first time old, lined, eighty years. Early one morning as the gray dawn began to appear under the stiff edge that the drawn curtain made at the window ledge, lightening the yellow pane of paper, the old rabbi in his sleep cried out, his eyes filling with tears, "No! No!" His hand clutched at his beard, tearing it as if mourning. He was ripping at his coat and shirt. "No more!"

"It's over," his wife called out, trying gently to shake him from the dream. "It's over."

"No," said the rabbi, wide awake, looking into her eyes. "No."

The carriage left Germany. Somewhere on the outskirts of Paris the rabbi pulled up the curtain and they looked out on green fields and rustic cottages. In the French capital clean-shaven men in velvet-collared coats came to the train to welcome them. He was given a room to stay in for several weeks that was all gold, a house filled with statues and paintings, where uniforms bowed to them, speaking another language. He was petted, filled with sweets, taught strange words for familar things, *bonbon, glacé, éclair, monsieur, mademoiselle* . . .

And though he passed from the cabin of a luxury liner to the modest deck of a three-family in the Bronx, the cradle in which the rabbi's son slept scarcely rocked. America, its vast spaces, were enclosed in the comfortable rooms smelling of the same chicken fat, stewed carrots, stuffed cabbage as Bohost. The students at the school he attended were like his playmates at home. English was quickly mastered, a game sweetened with rewards.

At school the son of the rabbi of Bohost, he was a favored child. If he paused before an answer, no one raised their voice to him, yanked him out of his seat, screaming, "Idiot! Blockhead!" No half-crazy old woman for his Hebrew teacher, hitting him on the head with the five books of Moses, shouting as she kicked him, "Pay attention!" He was never made fun of in front of the class, pointed out by the voice at the front, "Look at the stupid one. Look! Look! Stop mumbling, stand up, show yourself off, *pisherkeh*. You make in your pants yet?"

He never had to dig his pen deep into the oak top of the dest, carving his heart into it, cutting the channels of an imaginary river that would carry him off into another country where he might understand the language.

A book sailed down the aisle and smashed Harvey Blatz silly. If the son of the rabbi stared through the windows of the yeshivah rather than at the text before him, his teachers smiled and looked to another student. The Lux boy could start up from his dream and answer the question. Hebrew was a second tongue to him. He had learned it at home in songs and riddles. It was not a sack of incomprehensible words hurled to learn by rote. A smack of the ruler ready to catch him at the first mistake. Hebrew vowels swarmed around Harvey's head, bees, the consonants, a fire of thorns. He was beset on all sides.

No question of payment for the rabbi's child. The yeshivah, honored to have him in attendance, refused to accept the fee. They insisted it would disgrace them to take money from a scholar. In Dorchester, week after week, Harvey was humiliated in front of his classmates. His mother could not pay the lump sum for Hebrew school tuition. It was agreed that it should come in small weekly installments.

"You think I'll pay for this *dreck?*" asked Jacob Blatz, picking Harvey's Hebrew book up from the kitchen table.

"Put it down," snapped Mrs. Blatz. "Fast!"

"A bunch of *bubemeisers.*" He was holding the worn copy up in the air. "Look." He tore a page out, blew his nose in it.

"Fast!" screamed Mrs. Blatz.

"Fast!" he shouted, throwing the book at Harvey, who was in tears. "Do things fast! Fast in this house." He stomped out while the boy bent down to try smoothing out the crumpled page, putting it back in the book. At night Mrs. Blatz would go through the limp pants hanging on the bedstead looking for the fee. She could barely slip enough out of Jacob's wallet to pay for groceries and rent. Several weeks she sent Harvey in with a box from Jake's stock of socks to cover the installment.

"*Nu,* what's this?" his teacher called out. She held up a long green sock, the color running through it in sun-faded streaks. She put her hand in. A finger came out a hole in the toe. She drew it toward her nose, which wrinkled.

"Ecccch! A joke?" Rushing down the aisle, the

woman grabbed Harvey's nostrils between the green web of her glove, stuffed it up.

Taunted, jeered, bull's-eye of every spitball, butt of gum on the seat, ink down the back, coat hiding, wallet lifting, desk filled with rubbish, a toe half the class accidentally stepped on. If Harvey cried, it was worse. They threw chalk at him, erasers, sang dirty songs:

> There's a brown spot
> Upon your nose
> And every day it
> Grows and growwwwwwwws.

He tried to grin through the chorus. Everyone burst into laughter. "What's up?" screamed the teacher. "Fishwitz, how come you're laughing?"

"Harvey made me," piped Fishwitz.

The teacher, looking down at Harvey's hysterical grin, went crazy, threw her blotter at him, her purse, the papers on her desk. She raged down the aisle and battered him under his desk.

A shy smile crept onto the lips of the Lux boy. Made much of by teachers, parents, schoolmates, he shared the treats of his lunchbag, was always ready to help another with homework, brought many to his house for supper—a prince.

Perhaps he was as unfortunate as Harvey. What does a prince know of his playfellows? They are always on best behavior. Children learn with fists and kicks how the world goes. While the Lux boy hurried home to his mother, most of the yeshivah kids lingered behind in the schoolyard, gutter, rubbing up against one another, swearing friendships, making enemies, haggling, cheating, telling lies, swapping practical know-how. They set off to steal apples, light fires, discussed girls, were beaten up by toughs, got a taste of sweet and sour beyond the book margin. Even Harvey learned—hopping from fence top to fence top in the backyards on the way home from Hebrew school, chased by a kid yipping, "Kill him! Kill him!"

The rabbi was not prepared. On his seventeenth birthday both parents were killed.

He was in school when it happened. The teachers called him out, ushered him into the principal's office. The head of the yeshivah, a friend of his father's, sat him down, began to tell a story of a young boy to whom the Almighty entrusts two precious jewels (yes, that well-polished old chestnut), how the gleaming things are only for a while. One day He calls to take them back. They wiled away tears with a dozen such tales of fortitude, calm acceptance, goodwill in the face of the Angel.

In their clumsy comforting they tread underfoot the dictums of Talmud, breaking those fragile reeds which carry a man over the floods. Rejoice, they murmured, a saint, your father goes to Heaven in white, flowing robes. They distracted him so that he could not tear his garments to the skin in the first flush of grief. They should have hit him between the eyes, a heavy beam, stunned and fallen quiet. "Sigh in silence!" Ezekiel XXIV: 17. Even the incompetents who went to comfort Job knew better. "They sat down with him upon the ground seven days and seven nights, and none spoke a word unto him: for they saw that his grief was very great." It was not a time for comfort but affliction. Overturn the benches, sit low on the floor, unshaven, unbathed, make yourself sick. "A mourner during the first three days should look upon himself as if a sword pricked between his shoulders." Moed Katan.

Had the boy torn his hair, screamed, fallen with clenched teeth to the floor, he might have been spared. Consolation? Woe, God cries to Job's comforters, "I'm angry. You didn't speak the truth of me."

Job, Job was blessed for his hideous lament.

"Why? Why?"

Would you believe that Rabbi Lux had been a child of nightmares? That despite the warm mantle of kisses and hugs his parents threw over the bed each night, as soon as they left, the lights out, a host of monsters came swarming from the closet, looming over the bedposts, chill demons, ogres, grisly shapes with chattering teeth. Death, coarse-haired and red, comes grinning among them, till the boy called out frantic and brought his mother bursting through the darkness to his side. The more beautiful the garden, the uglier its serpent, lurking.

Now he closed the door on that closet. He had to be a man. He turned with his smile, unearthly, to the world. All was for the best. He would believe only in goodness. He followed in his father's footsteps, training for the rabbinate, but also attended, as was the Bohosta's wish, an American college. Between one and the other, he had little time to think about himself. Completing studies, he took charge of a synagogue, a thriving one in the center of our community. Beth Rachmoniss was beset with so many problems, he never took stock of his own.

From a babe he became an elder of Israel. The closet remained locked. According to legend, the preserver of Judaism, Yohanan ben Zakkai, spent 40 years in business, 40 years in study, before he began to give advice. Something was missing in Rabbi Lux's background. He looked fondly at the teenagers in his congregation but was at a loss for words. What could he say to young Blatz? How could he understand the problem?

Yet 4,000 years, self-imposed, of cultivating a particular trait links us Jews. We all have it in common. Though the bloods of a thousand races run in our veins. Those who cleave to the family become as one.

Twin strands gently descending, looping, circling an invisible pole of ancestry in whose flesh succeeding generations have graven behavior. What memory of horror is carried down them? Enough to twine the rabbi into Harvey's arms.

Let us take up the burden of the story again, the moment when Rabbi Lux struggled up out of his bed from under the weight of the dark bag, the corpse, his wife, the blankets.

CHAPTER TEN

IN WONDERLAND

FROM such dreams Rabbi Lux fled to a seat of refuge among the high places. He squatted on the white porcelain bowl of his panacea and sought aid.

He came to flush his bowels. Does not Isaiah cry out, "Behold, O Lord: for I am in distress, my bowels are troubled." Previously the rabbi had been able to ease himself of the sickness within. Now his system balked. Instead of the sphincters' relaxing and letting go, they held on. Lux turned and twisted on the seat, miserable. "Mine eyes do fail with tears, my bowels are troubled, my liver is poured upon the earth."

He was reciting Isaiah on the toilet. A forbidden act. You are not supposed to dwell on holy thoughts when you relieve yourself. You are not allowed to dwell on the Law there. Not a fit seat of judgment. Yet Rabbi Lux found himself helpless. Questions kept popping into his mind. He couldn't get off the seat. He was right in the middle of . . .

Psalms, bits of the Proverbs, difficult passages of Talmud kept occurring to him as he sat and strained. He tried desperately to drive them out of his mind, shaking his head back and forth to confuse his brains.

Mocking him, questions of clean and unclean presented themselves, demanding a decision. They whispered in his ear. He put his finger in the drums. They danced before his eyes. He shut his lids tight. They flew into his nose. Before he could sneeze, they buzzed in his brain. Caught, he couldn't pray, not with his filth still on him. Yet he couldn't get up (not in the middle) to wash his hands and make himself clean. In such a state of impurity he did not dare to open his lips and call for assistance on the Divine Name. How long? he wept. How long before his bowels relented? The smell of offal came up from the bowl, stank in his nostrils. His own smell turned his stomach, made him sicker.

Was there such a case before? He could not avoid a legal examination, although in this place it was void and blasphemous. Was there a precedent?

An evil train of thought. It brought him to Job. (Don't! He couldn't help.) Job had been struck, and picked up his own dung to scrape himself. Had he prayed? He cursed. He cursed the day of his birth.

The stench from the bowl was putrescent. Boils. Job had cursed the womb that bore him. How could you curse your mother? His own, a sweet, mild woman. To curse her womb? Did it extend to the seed that created you? His father? Please! It wasn't right to think of your parents here. They're dead, one recalls them with the phrase of "blessed memory." Only curses were appropriate in this place.

"Stop it! Stop!" Rabbi Lux cried. His mind was wandering into rabbinical jurisprudence. It was madness, yet he couldn't stop. Did he have any curses to utter against his parents? If the sage Shammai was right and it was better the world had never been created, was it better his father had never spilled seed into his mother? Was he to blame? No! No! The world was a beautiful place. Blessed be his father for creating him.

Oy! You weren't supposed to bless in this position. Rabbi Lux swore. Did he look, did he smell beautiful? If the world was wonderful, what was disturbing him? Maybe the trouble was with him. Maybe he was a flawed vessel. Should he bless his parents for creating such a thing? He was cursed.

"Aaaaah! Aaaaaaaaaah!" Rabbi Lux rose up from the seat for a moment to shake off these thoughts. He sank back onto it in despair as he felt a loose tickle stir under him. He had to stay in his place. He nodded back and forth on the tacky enamel until he realized he was falling into the rhythm of prayer. Impious. Exhausted, he leaned pack on the pipes of the water cabinet and began to doze. Sleep . . . Sleep . . .

Slowly Rabbi Lux felt the rim of the toilet, a flaking wooden horseshoe, begin to stretch under him. It pulled at the flesh of his buttocks painfully as the horseshoe's inner circumference grew larger and larger. With a rip, his bottom came away from the seat and he began to slide down.

"Return, return, all you backsliding children," a voice cried. Lux tried to expand his buttocks, to raise himself back on the seat. "All but Lux!" the voice announced. A hand pushed. He slid. The smooth porcelain sent a chill through him. He splashed into warm water.

"Eccccch!" The filth in the porcelain bowl bobbed around. The rabbi pushed it away. He had prayed for water to wash his hands. This was pollution. He dog-paddled desperately through the stuff toward the shiny white sides. It clotted in his eyes, mouth, nose. The chamber grew larger, the sides retreated further and further. The top loomed higher and higher. A wind began to howl in the cave. It churned waves in his face. The tepid waters overwhelmed him, closing over his head. Heavy and bilious, he sank down, down, a dead weight. "My flesh is worms," thought Rabbi Lux. "My clothes abhor me." He opened his mouth, rottenness. "He that goes down to the pit shall come up no more." Mercifully he was stifled in darkness.

Steady, incessant, pounding, above him, the waters knocked. His clothes were clammy, his hair wet. His fingers gripping a tiny ledge of rock, smarted. He pressed his body in close against the damp wall. The rock kept crumbling away in pebbles underneath, his toes slipping as he tried to find a firm foothold.

The tips of his fingers ached. His head throbbed. A cramp was bending his chest in two. How long? How long?

"Heee heee heeee!" A shrill laugh rang in his ear. "Lo, though I walk through the valley . . . hee hee hee . . ."

"Hello? Hello?" asked Rabbi Lux.

"Lost yer way, Hahvey?"

"I'm not Hahvey."

"No, yer St. Patrick."

"Could you tell me where I am?"

"All roight, get a move on it. Don't be hangin' around here."

"Hee hee heee . . ."

"Come on, me bucko, get down off that wall!"

"I can't. . . ."

"Listen, Blatz, Oi'm tired of runnin' all over hell lookin' fer you. Look at yer face! Filthy dirty and covered with pimples. Come on, the rabbi's lookin' fer you, too."

"I can't."

"C'mon, yer a sissy. Jump! Jump!"

"Oooowwwww! Ooooowwww!"

"All roight, y'only skinned yer knee. If you go climbin' up the puddin' stone here in Franklin Park, you've only yerself t'blame on the way down. Wipe yer stupid-lookin' face and let's be goin'. Oi'm not on overtime fer the lost-boys detail."

A hot, fat tear oozed out of his eye and trickled, tickling, down his bumpy cheek. He put up a hand to brush it away.

"Don't pick yer pimples, thay'll niver go away!"

Sniffling, he put his finger to his leaky nose.

"Oh! Get it away from there, too! Y'll disfigure that puss. Y'll niver git on the force. Y'll niver qualify. Come on, pick yerself up. Brush that dirt off yer pants. Give me yer little paw. Thay're we go, I knew you had a bit of sense in that thick skull. I bet the rabbi is lookin' fer you in the moonkey cage. Let's be walkin' over."

The red-faced policeman with yellow stripes pulled him along. The officer's hand was hairy, tufts of scarlet wool spilled out from under the blue cuff of his uniform, sprouted down his fingers to curling nails. Tiny warts splotched the policeman's hand. Horny, they rubbed into his soft palm as the sergeant squeezed it. The crimson-splashed face of the policeman looked down. "Oi've got eczema meself. Very unpleasant, isn't it?"

"It's all right."

"Oh, is it?" The face of the sergeant flushed a terrible purple. "Let me have one of those pimples of yers. All roight? We'll see how you like it. There! There! We'll squeeze it a bit."

"Owwwww! Owwwww!"

A warm trickle started down his leg, burning the skin. A little puddle under his foot.

"Oh, Holy Saints! How old are you?"

"Fourteen . . ."

"Fourteen, eh? And still can't hold on to yer bladder. Come on, I want to get you over to that moonkey cage. Y'll niver make the police force."

Yanked along, he stumbled down a trail full of holes and large rocks. It was damp and foggy. On either side in the mists, he could make out crumbling buildings. Growling and shrieks from them.

"You've ruined me uniform. Oi've a mind to throw you in the lion's cage."

Stinging drops gathered in his eyes.

"Heee heeee heeee . . ." The palm of the policeman felt shaggy and matted in his own. He looked up into a huge, hairy mouth. It stared down at him full of sharp-pointed teeth, breathing an odor of meat.

He closed his eyes and felt fingers grip his hand again. They stopped. A little man stood before them on the trail, holding a crumpled paper bag.

"Socks! Socks! Want cut-rate socks? Socks! Cashmere! Silk! Dacron! Cotton and wool! Burlap and linen! Socks!"

"How much are y'chargin', me boy?"

"Cheap! For you, ten dollars a pair."

"Yer off yer rocker. Where's yer license? Hey! Wait up! Wait up!"

The little man, barefooted, scrambled into the bushes with his paper bag. Ahead of them, from a hole in the trail, his head suddenly popped up. "You don't exist!"

"It's yer father!" shouted the policeman. "Catch him! Catch him! Step on his head! Oh, it's too late. I'll get you, Jakie," said the policeman standing over the hole in the trail. "I'll lock you up in the Springfield Nut House. No one the wiser. You'll niver get out!"

"The truth is," said the sergeant, bending back to his ear with a whisper, "Oi only humor him. He's not worth the trouble. He gave us a bit of fun for a while, but it was small potatoes. His own worst enemy."

"Yer the same. If the rabbi hadn't taken such a liken to you—Oi can't be chasin' all the fools in Dorchester—we'd have left you hangin' on that puddin' stone till kingdom come."

Throwing back his head, the policeman broke out into a falsetto:

"Oh the pray-ers of the pious
So sweet-ly descend
To the Lord's right-hand angel
They cheer-fully wend.

Here we are!"

They had come to the top of a rise in the trail. Down below, a stone building that looked like a miniature of the Roman Coliseum, ruined stone arches piled one on top of the other, sat squat in the midst of dead grasses. There were bars between the arches, although many of the iron struts were twisted into loops or broken off. Weeds thrust between the crisscrossed lines of the bars. And a fierce growth of poison ivy sprouted from the crumbling stone.

"Here we are at the moonkey cage. Now listen, Hahvey, you wait here, while Oi go in and see if the boys have seen the rabbi. Just linger by the door. Don't get scared and be runnin' off. It's a bit lonely since the apes broke out and ran away, but nothin' here to hurt you."

The sergeant extended his oak nightstick and whacked four times on the door. Then he whistled "Ha-Tickvoh" and blew his nose loudly. The door swung open and a sallow-faced old man with a black yarmulkah on stuck his head out. "*Nu?*"

"It's Abie's Irish rose!"

The old man nodded to the policeman, who strode in through the door. Through the open crack one saw a crowd of men. The fumes of their cigar smoke trailed in green clouds.

"Who are you looking for?"

"The rabbit."

"Lux?" Farts and belches burst through the room. "That *shmegegge!*"

"Shah!" cried a sharp voice. "The results are coming in from Suffolk Downs."

"Sarge," whispered a low voice, scraping up old phlegm as it sounded, "he's right dere." An enormous finger circled by a brass ring, 20-karat gold-plated, crooked in the fog. "Between duh peroxide's legs."

The green air swirled around a pale face, caked with purple rouge, a tousled mop of bleached-blond hair streaming down on each side and out of which, below, thrust a large tit's rosette. A soprano screeched, "He'd like to be. He wouldn't mind a piece of *tochis!* I got the same *zitsfleysh* as that Yehoodiss."

Giggles resounded in the smoke. "How'd duh *meshuggeneh?* Sarge, you get a piece of her?"

"She was a nympho!" screeched the sharp little voice.

A long tongue licked to appreciative murmurs.

A white patch fanned the air. It was a racing sheet and at the top of it, a black yarmulkah peeped over the edge. "You think he's here?" It was the sharp voice again, the one that had protested the noise. "Outside his study he knows nothing. With him, everything is fine. And that's all right with us.

"I'm worth a hundred thousand! I got children, seed, 12 grandchildren and the great-grandchildren are coming. A house in Dorchester, four stories. I can buy one in Newton anytime.

"Where is the rod of God? The book business is a golden bull. I'm screwing half of Dorchester everyday. The more I screw, the more business comes in. I grab dollars on every street corner along Blue Hill Avenue. And I got a flock of underlings collecting.

"I can stuff bucks into my kids' pockets until they dance. On this dough they're dancing to saxophones in Miami Beach, Palm Springs. This is prosperity. I'll die a happy man.

"You know what I say to God? '*Gay veck!*' Who needs you? What good do you do me? Who are you? Where's my profit? What'll you give me?

"You know where I made my money? I stole. I murdered. I took from widows, from kids without fathers or mothers, clothes right off a back. On Erie Street, on Lawrence Avenue, down the length of Blue Hill, they groan when I come with my boys to collect.

"I'll be punished, eh? When? Already I'm eighty. I'll be shoveled into an acre plot under a marble stone ten feet high, a happy man.

"Happy! Happy!" crooned the sharp little voice, imitating the soulful chant of a cantor. "Happy are those who live in your tents."

Applause sounded through the room. A plump, hairless white hand grasped the thin, bony claw under the yarmulkah, pumping it up and down. "Oh God, God wove you, what a thpeech! You're a real thcholar. What a head! A *chochem!* You're worth a thouthand Luxth. A thmuck, that wabbit. A parathite. Like you thaid, what doeth he know? A thoftie, a maggot."

The little white hand waved gaily in the air. "I'm a gueth of honor in hith thynagogue. Evewy Yom Kippur I pwedge a thouthand dollath. What a hand they give me. What a thmile the wabbi thwos. For nothing. Oooooooh! It knockth my eye out. For nothing. They never thee the dough. A thouthand dollath. He bewieveth it evewy time. He maked the congwegation bewieve it, too. What a thweetie! He bewieveth evewything."

"I believed you!" a hoarse voice shouted. It came from a pair of huge black eyes that were crossed and kept blinking. The whole room burst into screams of laughter.

"Why not? Who knowth? Howth the egg buthineth?"

"Golden," replied the eyeballs, blinking merrily. "Laying up and down Dorchester. Listen! Don't pick on the rabbit. A goose! A nice fellow. He sits put. Right? Okay?"

"What's he doing around here?" asked a big cigar puffing green smoke.

The red nose of the sergeant appeared next to the cigar. "He's lookin' fer Hahvey?"

"Harvey?"

"Hahvey Blatz."

"That *shmendrick* his father," shouted the blinking eyes, crossing and uncrossing, "ran away with a bag of my dough. He flew the coop on a collection. I'll wring his neck if I catch him."

"Hahveey, oooooh. He'th the boy I met in the thcoolyard on Nightingale Thtreet. He hath a nythe mouth."

The fat white hand bent to the side, girlish and coy. The room began to giggle. "He hath good thtrong lipth."

The fog shook with hilarity. "Yer a naughty boy," said the sergeant, winking. "Whad yuh do with him?"

"I wocked him up with the elephant."

"What?"

"He'th thucking!"

"Ha ha ha . . ." The room exploded with laughter, waves of it rocked through the green smoke, back and forth, until everyone was drowning in a whirlpool of glee. Round and round the noses, eyes, hands and ears spun, until suddenly everything was sucked down and the rabbi found himself standing inside a steep iron pipe staring down its incline at a disappearing stream.

The rabbi looked up. A few feet above his head was a manhole cover. He shivered. The pipe was warm but his clothes were clammy. Slowly, inch by inch, he crept up till his hand touched the cold surface of the manhole cover. Pushing with all his strength, sweating and straining against the heavy iron circle, he began to lift it out of its slot. The slab swung up and rolled to the side.

A mouth stared at him from the top of the hole. Rotting meat reeking. A row of ivory spikes like palisades glittered in the light. The orifice over the hole opened wide and at the very back the rabbi could see a bell-shaped tissue trembling and shaking. The black nose of the lion bristled with whiskers as thick as nails.

A dull roar sounded under the rabbi. He looked down to see a green tide fast rising in the pipe. It surged against his ankles when a pink rug rolled to him. Gratefully he scrambled onto it. The tongue flicked up, high in the air, and the rabbi sprang down its soft slope.

The lion began to move. A gentle, almost imperceptible rocking. Anxious to see where they were going, Rabbi Lux pitched forward on his hands and knees, began to crawl up the soft pile.

On the tip of the beast's tongue the rabbi looked through milky teeth. He was in the lion's cage. Across the way there was another pen. An elephant lay in it. The creature was on its back and there were a number of women dressed in dungarees or pedal pushers standing around it. Some were trying to force a huge oversized cookie into its mouth, while others were fastening its bands. They had tied the elephant down on its side with iron chains. The rabbi recognized members of the Sisterhood of Temple Beth Rachmoniss. There were electrodes attached to the body of the elephant. They were giving it shock treatment. A crazy elephant? One of the women, an old lady, stumbled around the group—asking, "Ready? *Nu?* Ready?"

No one paid any attention to her. Finally, on her own, she hobbled over to the side of the pen and pulled a switch. The elephant screamed and began to tremble and jerk in its chains. Its trunk twisted at the pegs and trumpeted forth piteous moans. It turned huge black eyes on the rabbi and bleated forth in a deafening cry. Rabbi Lux recognized it. Yehoodiss! Yehoodiss!

The lion sprang up in the cage, roaring. The rabbi was hurled back down the carpet. He clutched at the bell-shaped tissue before he could be swept down the beast's trachea. As the chamber underneath him became stable again, he dropped off and crawled quickly back on the tongue to the light.

They were no longer in the zoo. Looking through the lion's teeth, the rabbi saw sand all around him. Dunes of gold stretched to the right and left of the beast's path. It was climbing a hill. Rabbi Lux saw smoke rising from the other side. The animal slouched slowly forward. As it rose over the top of the rise and began to descend, the rabbi discovered the origin of the smoke. Eight or nine men were sitting around a campfire. In the distance, across the trackless waste, a police wagon was speeding off.

So intent were the men on their own affairs, laughing, that the lion was only a few feet away when their chatter stopped. Those with their backs to the animal saw its reflection in the eyes across from them.

No one at the campfire moved. "Please," an old man in a high silk hat with his back to the lion began to whimper, "we didn't do nothing bad. Don't hurt us. Please!"

"All right?" whimpered a little cockeyed man opposite him. In a tiny voice he begged, "Okay?"

Rabbi Lux was startled to recognize the high silk hat. It belonged to the president of his synagogue. The man with the crossed eyes was a member of the *shul*, too. The cantor was sitting beside him. A fruit man who was in Beth Rachmoniss, a shopkeeper, and several other members of its board of directors were squatting by the fire. The rabbi stuck his head through the lion's open teeth and called out, "Hello!"

The men, not daring to move, craned their heads up in amazement. "It's you?" they said together in a whisper.

"What's going on?" asked the rabbi. "Nobody notified me of the meeting. Something important?"

"Nothing," they replied in chorus.

"Maybe you can help me?" he asked, stretching out a little further.

"Sure!" they assented in one voice.

"Have you seen Harvey? Harvey Blatz?"

A snicker went around the campfire. With a foolish smile on his face, the president turned around. "We just sold him."

"Sold him?"

"They needed someone, Egypt."

"Sold him?"

The lion started up, standing on its hind legs, rolling Rabbi Lux under its tongue. It let out a growl. The circle of men shook. Falling on his face, the president, his high silk hat in the dust, began nervously to try and propitiate the beast. "Please," he said in a dry, scratched voice, "someone had to go. We had to send someone. It's a law. So many each year. You want us to send the boys that are college material? This one is a dropout for sure. Not even healthy. Full of pimples. Nutty, too. We thought we pulled a good deal on them. Listen, we stuck them with a bad one. Who would you want to go?"

"Yeah, yeah. All right," piped up the small man with crossed eyes. The lion's raised paw cut him off.

Rabbi Lux peeped out again from under the beast's tongue. "Where's he going?"

The president pointed to the black dot of the police wagon, now far away. "They took him for a physical."

"He's in with the hoods from Eastie," squeaked his echo. "South Boston, too."

The lion tightened its lips around the rabbi. Arching its back, it sprang off its haunches and broke into a gallop toward the black dot.

Sand flew all around them. The rabbi had to wiggle back to avoid the stinging dust. Slowly the dot of the paddy wagon grew larger. The lion, almost upon it, paused in midair and came bolting down.

Stepping out, the rabbi, gingerly, began to descend. At the bottom of the tongue he saw—. The rabbi hurried forward.

The body was face down in the sand. He turned it over. The boy's face was beaten, a pudding, white flesh streaked with blood. Harvey was limp. Jelly trickled out of his ears. Pinned to the breast was a piece of paper, a printed form.

4 F

FLUNKED HIS PHYSICAL

The rabbi picked the child up in his arms. He turned around to the lion. The beast was gone. He and the corpse were abandoned in the middle of the desert. The rabbi felt his heart grow bitter. The salt in the air parched his throat. The stomach juices came up on his tongue. A draught of urine. He began to cough and cchhhhuppp, to empty the sourness. His breath flared. Phlegm gathered and gathered, no matter how often he spat. He wanted to pray over the boy, but his lips were hot, poisonous. "Let me swallow down my spittle." He remembered the line. "My bowels boil within me. . . . What have I done to you?"

"Our Father, our Father," he chanted on his cracked lips, trying to begin. A cloud of dust rose from the desert floor. It blew in his eyes, his mouth. In the whirling sand his father appeared. A corpse, the dignified beard had withered to a few wisps of gray thread. The flesh still hung on the skull, but it had flaked away to gleaming bone in spots. The wind blew through the hollow of his father's mouth. "The Law . . . the Law . . ." it whistled, dry and solemn.

Rabbi Lux held out the body. He shook the limp child in his arms. The old Bohosta held up a finger bone.

"Man is a worm," cried the wind in the skull. Hoarsely it insisted. "His son, a maggot."

Clutching the body of Harvey to him, Rabbi Lux shook his head. "No! No!"

"Our Father, our Father," he sang in terror as the corpse of the Bohosta broke into fragments. It wasn't fair. It wasn't fair. He ran forward holding the corpse of Harvey. "Our Father, our King, our Redeemer," he implored.

As Rabbi Lux staggered hugging the corpse, dunes on either side came closer and closer. Soon, as his eyes fell from the Heavens, he realized that he was heading into a valley. Something aching bright shone at the end of it, glittered like a heap of ivory. Gathering up the last strength of his bowels, Rabbi Lux rushed as fast as he could toward the brilliance. He had to shield his eyes. It hurt to look directly at it.

No! As he came to the foot of the flaming whiteness, Rabbi Lux looked up to see the sun's reflection on a great heap of bones. The empty rib cages of beasts. Skulls hundreds of feet wide that must have housed the brains of monsters. Jaws that could have swallowed tall buildings. A single tooth that rested in the bottom of the valley but whose edge glistened at the crest of the dune thousands of feet above. Thousands, millions, uncountable bones stretched back on top of one another into an endless valley, the very floor of which was a moldering pile of them. Bleached, they shone in the sun though cobwebs thick as silk lay over all.

Who presided here? Was he to leave the body?

In front of the heap Rabbi Lux saw the skeleton of his father. It's mouth was distended in a crooked smile. It perched on the ribs of an elephant, grinning.

Rabbi Lux called out in the valley, "Hello? Hello?"

"Shhhhhhhh . . . Shhhhhhhh . . ." The Irish cop stood at his ear smiling hugely with a flaring, crimson face.

Rabbi Lux turned around and asked softly, "Please, please . . ."

"Thhhhhh . . . Thhhhh . . ." A politician with cheeks of dark purple stood beside the rabbi's other ear. He held a finger to oily lips and lisped, "Thhhhhhhhhh . . ."

The sound shivered through the valley, rocking the bones. It whistled in the rabbi's ears till his head spun. He looked up and a flood of water was rising over the dunes. A green tidal wave, its crest curled in the air, foaming with familiar houses, wife beaters, shakedown artists, gamblers and cheats. Then it broke over the top and streamed down, bearing Dorchester in churning surf. As the spray hit the rabbi's face, he looked down at Harvey and cried:

"Shhhhhh . . . Shhhhhhh . . . Shhhhhh . . ."

The toilet bowl overflowed under Rabbi Lux. He had flushed it in his dozing till the spring broke.

He awoke to find himself wet and with a chapped, red buttock.

CHAPTER ELEVEN

FIRST STEPS

FROM his dreams the rabbi stumbled off to the synagogue—and the community. Ah, the community! We left its members telling dirty stories about Yehoodiss. Well, the community was in for a shock.

Rabbi Lux? Who expected it from Rabbi Lux? A meek and forgiving man, the congregation had stepped on him for years.

At first they only noticed that something was erratic. His shirts, or shirt, gave off a stale odor. And the collar cuffs had gone limp, gray; the front, spotted, streaked. His black suit wrinkled on him, went shiny at the knees, elbows, hung like a sack. The kindly full flesh of his face was melting away. Bones, harsh, angular, thrust out. The nose, that little dumpling, became a hook, sharp, accusing. Those eyes, so soft, shy, like deer hiding from everyone, now stared vacantly ahead, or bolted suddenly into your face to knock you over. People looked away nervously.

His gait—he started to rush down the corridors of the synagogue, stopped abruptly, wheeled around, began to pull at his hair until it was sticking out in all directions, a wild man's.

Each week he was thinner, paler than the last; his attention more easily distracted. He mumbled during half the service and during the other half he would shake as if a fit were coming upon him.

The cantor and the president of the *shul*, who were up on the altar with Lux, saw that the sweat stood out on his forehead in large, transparent tears. He kept dropping the prayer book. His eyes were red and feverish. "Anything the matter?" they asked casually. He shook his head. Later they remarked that the rest of him was shaking, too.

Yet it was not the rabbi's physical condition that worried the congregation and its leaders. Man is as the grass that withers. Here today and gone tomorrow. If it's time for him to go, they reasoned, it's time for him to go. No—it wasn't his disintegrating health that upset them. It was his behavior in the pulpit.

In the middle of a sermon on human kindness—a pious talk full of the rabbi's usual sweetness and forbearance, "Love thy neighbor as thyself," that was the theme and it was embroidered with a thousand examples from the Talmud, a witty yet wholesome sermon and one he wasn't giving for the first time—he starts to mumble. Then he cries from the pulpit, "Crazy Fishelson, you beat your wife!"

The congregation shook their heads. The rabbi is supposed to talk from the Torah. Is Crazy Fishelson in the Torah? They misheard. But Fishelson turns white in the face, right where he is sitting. The rabbi? The rabbi is sweating. He's in a fever. But he starts to mumble again. And then he leans forward. Looks right out into the congregation. Right at Fishelson the fruit man. With a shaking hand the rabbi shouts, "Stand up, Fishelson!"

Poor Fishelson. He can't look the rabbi in the face. And the rabbi cries out, "A disgrace before the community. An offense to God."

Fishelson stood up shaking. "Who? . . . What ???" he mumbled, confused and frightened.

"Don't do it!" shouted the rabbi.

Fishelson looked to his friends for help. But the men in the pews looked away from him. They were amazed. They knew he beat his wife. It was common knowledge in Fishelson's part of Dorchester. In fact, they laughed about it. It was funny to see Mrs. Fishelson running down the street, from door to door, with Crazy Fishelson chasing after, shouting he'd give her a bloody *tochis.* He enjoyed it himself. But to hear it from the bema. From the mouth of the rabbi. It wasn't so funny. Fishelson, a big man, who could tear a telephone book in two, a man who contributed more than his share to keep Beth Rachmoniss going, opened his mouth to explain.

"Shaaaaahh!" shouted the rabbi. "Lying! An abomination to the Lord. Don't do it! You know what I mean. Leave her alone, Fishelson!"

Fishelson backed out of his pew. "Rabbi . . ." he said, trying to get a word in.

"Fishelson?" cried the rabbi. "Job! 'Shall vain words have an end?' Out! Out! And don't come back till your wife comes and begs for you."

So Crazy Fishelson was driven from the synagogue. An event! Well, after so many years, reasoned the congregation, the rabbi was entitled to one burst of anger. The old men scratched at their beards as the fruit man fled down the aisle and out into the street. In the ladies' section there were a few murmurs of approval.

A rough way to deal with someone. But to beat your wife—it's not right. A lot of hats bobbed sanctimoniously.

Up on the bema the president rubbed his fingers into his white silk yarmulkah. Fishelson didn't contribute that much to Beth Rachmoniss. He wasn't so important, either. The fruit men are not a very powerful group in Dorchester. And Fishelson had made a lot of enemies, slipping rotten fruit into the bottom of the bag. Just the other week the president remembered with acid a rancid tangerine. Let him taste a little bitterness. As for Fishelson's neighbors, they were ashamed to make a fuss. They had stood by while he beat his wife. Not a friend would stir for him.

So the incident was smoothed over. Fishelson went home cursing. He swore at his wife. But he didn't beat her. What should happen three weeks later? Mrs. Fishelson comes to the synagogue to see the rabbi. Let her husband come back to *shul,* she weeps. And Fishelson himself is standing, penitent, outside the rabbi's door. A sin offering, a bag of sweet Israeli oranges in hand.

But meanwhile. As Fishelson left the synagogue that day, the rabbi almost collapsed on the bema. No sooner had the fruit man gone through the rear door than the rabbi's face broke out in sweat. He put his face in his hands and, muttering, "Excuse me, please . . . excuse me . . ." fled from the altar at Beth Rachmoniss, locking himself in his office until services were over. Not even the janitor saw him. Rabbi Lux exited through a side door and rushed home, incognito.

The next few days at the synagogue the rabbi refused to look anyone in the face. He went about his business with his head down, talking to himself. They were afraid to mention it to him. Obviously he was disturbed about the incident. Well, let a dead dog lie. It wasn't going to happen again. He was ashamed of the affair. It was best that everyone forget about it. No apologies. Nothing.

Then, two weeks later, right in the middle of the Eighteen Benedictions, when the cantor comes to the chant, "Satisfy us, O Lord, out of thy goodness, thy bounty . . ." Rabbi Lux jumps up, turns to the president and cries, "Where is your bounty? Your goodness? You burned up the Torah coverings. Now the Queen comes out of the ark in rags!"

"Wha . . ." says the president, amazed, putting his hands on his head.

"Your head," shouts the rabbi, "you cover with silk. You can cover your head with white silk before God. And you dressed His words in a *shmatte*. You think He doesn't spit on you? When are you going to pay . . .?"

"A mistake . . . you understood . . . a mistake . . ." stammered the surprised president from his seat beside the holy ark on the altar.

The whole congregation began to buzz. The rabbi was speaking in such a loud voice that they could all hear. "Then *rectify!*" snapped the rabbi at the president. "A mistake? If it stands another day it's a sin. If the Torah comes out of the ark next Sabbath in that cloth you burned, I'll wrap it around you. For a shroud at your funeral. Right now, before the whole congregation, make a pledge—500 dollars for a new wrapping. Up and make a pledge!"

The president, a man not usually at a loss for words, got up from his seat beside the ark. He was astonished. He got up from the carved wooden throne that stood to the rabbi's own chair and stammered to the congregation, "Look . . . it's a bad year in gabardine. . . . I can't afford . . ."

"To the grave can you take it with you?" interjected the rabbi. "Shall I put it in your box—the bags from the First National? They'll keep you company? How many years have you got? While you can, make good!"

At these words the president began to feel dizzy. Every day he worried about how many years he would have. Every time they said the Mourner's Kaddish in *shul,* he thought next time for me. The rabbi's warning went straight to his heart. He felt palpitations. His knees gave way. He would have an attack, right on the bema. "Please . . . please . . ." he begged as he tried to sit.

The rabbi caught him by the arm. "Make a pledge!" he insisted, holding the old man up.

"I'll make it . . ." wheezed the president.

"Make it!"

"I'm making . . ."

The rabbi let the old president fall back into his seat. He strode up to the altar where the cantor was still singing (although in a voice low enough so that he and everyone else in the *shul* could hear what was going on). Interrupting the service, Rabbi Lux announced that the president had just pledged 500 dollars.

Now the congregation really had something to buzz about. Everybody was talking at once. The service was forgotten. The cantor, for instance, had closed his book and was looking with a grin at the president. The poor man had a hand on his chest and was breathing with difficulty. The cantor didn't make his breath come any easier. He leered into the old man's face, mocking him. The cantor's lips puckered in smug triumph. Miser, thief, he sang silently.

Rabbi Lux turned around and saw the cantor. Stiffening, he walked up to the young man. He extended his arm. The cantor smiled broadly and put out his own arm for a confidential handshake. The president had paid. What was his surprise to feel the rabbi's hand go to his cheek instead. The rabbi was pinching his cheek. Pinch! The blood came into his right eye. His whole face winced. The cantor put out his arm to push the rabbi away when the latter shouted, "Five hundred dollars!" At that moment the old president fell forward out of his chair in what looked like a heart attack. But hardly anyone noticed it. Because Rabbi Lux suddenly doubled up as in pain and wailed aloud. Oy! Rabbi Lux staggered off the bema of Beth Rachmoniss, out of the hall, down the stairs and into the men's room in the basement. The vice-president and the *shummus* had to finish the prayers. He stayed locked in a stall until after the service and long after everyone had gone home. No one bothered him. Nobody wanted to talk to him there.

What to do? Nobody knew. A check arrived at Beth Rachmoniss from the hospital the next Tuesday—500 dollars. They had taken the president to the Beth Israel Hospital. His condition was diagnosed as indigestion, too much horseradish on his gefilte fish. Nevertheless, he called for an oxygen tent, a room in the isolation ward, a special dietitian, all the trimmings. He was staying there for a month, he told them. Let them check everything.

Was he mad at Beth Rachmoniss? That's what the congregation wanted to know. They didn't want to lose the King of Gabardine—not while he was alive. Was he mad at Rabbi Lux? No one could tell. The rabbi went to visit him in the hospital. What did they say to each other? The president put on an oxygen mask when the rabbi walked into his room every day. What kind of conversation could you hold like that? Yet the president received him. And he hadn't resigned yet. His check had come in for 500 dollars. It didn't bounce. Should they talk to the rabbi or not?

CHAPTER TWELVE

STREETWALKING

WHILE they debated whether to talk or not to talk, the board of Beth Rachmoniss, the bookies, numbers men, pool-room owners and etcetera who stood behind the synagogue supporting; while these latter-day props of the temple met informally in the back of Yehoodi's Pool Room and Taxi Stand to debate the fate of Rabbi Lux—the rabbi himself was not quiet.

No—the rabbi was in a fever. Whereas after the incident with Crazy Fishelson he had talked to no one, after the outbreak with the president he talked to everyone. Before, he had hidden at home and in his office, walking with a bowed head and hiding his face from the glance of Dorchester. Now he was out in the street lifting his face up and looking everyone in the eye. He didn't keep regular hours at the synagogue anymore but could be seen on Blue Hill Avenue and its side streets daily, seeking out the members of his synagogue.

"*Why* don't he stay in *shul?*" shouted Harry Shot of Hot Shot's Discount Den, a clearance-sale store that had expanded into the largest on Blue Hill Avenue in the last ten years. Harry burst into the Beth Rachmoniss board meeting in the back of Yehoodi's and shook his fist in the face of Cockeyed Zitzz, a bookie who was treasurer of the synagogue. "Keep him at home!" cried Harry, sticking his angry finger up Zitzz's nose. "You get my point?"

The point was that Rabbi Lux had shown up at the discount house one afternoon when Harry and two of his salesmen were about to sell a load of bad furniture and faulty appliances to a poor black couple, newly wedded, who were moving into a house in Dorchester.

"It was a big kill!" Harry Shot shouted in the faces of the board of Beth Rachmoniss. "A two-thousand-dollar sale!" Harry's own face, round and smooth-shaven, grew pink with anger. His pig nose wiggled furiously. His sales finger trembled under Zitzz's snout. "What is he, the Better Business Bureau?"

Two thousand dollars out the window! They had signed up those two *shvartzers* for everything. It was a big deal. The furniture and appliance salesmen got together and were really pulling the cotton over the couple's eyes. Harry himself had come over to make sure it was sown up right.

"What a couch," Harry was enthusing. Five foot two, he bounced with delight, turning his most fatherly and confidential smile on the young couple. "One of a kind! Custom-made. Foam rubber. Inner springs. A fabric that will last—indestructible—forever. Shit on it. Piss on it. Stamp on it. It stands up. It never fades. The color! Decorator-designed. The best in the store."

Harry pointed a finger at the couch. He turned with a sour face to the furniture salesman. "You really gave them a deal. At that price—they're stealing it from me." Turning back to the couple, Harry smiled. "It's all right. Be happy!" Rising on tiptoes, Harry winked at the husband and pulled the bride down to give her a kiss. He lifted his eyebrows and was reaching for a pen for them to sign—when to his amazement he beheld Rabbi Lux staring balefully at him from between two cartons. "Rabbi . . . ?" Harry asked, caught off guard.

Rabbi Lux, dressed in his black rabbinical suit and hat, stepped from between the cartons. He looked at Harry sadly, shook his head and then bent over the couch. Before Harry could shout, "Don't touch!" the awful sound of ripping material was heard. Rabbi Lux had pinched the couch. The fabric in which it was upholstered was like cheesecloth. And instead of foam rubber, a torrent of sawdust spilled out.

"Wha . . . ? Wha . . . ?" Harry couldn't even get the question out. What are you doing? And before they could stop him, Rabbi Lux had sat down in the red leather chair, one of a set of four that the couple had bought to go with the couch. This time it wasn't just that the genuine leather tore like plastic contact paper, but the wrought-iron legs snapped where they had been glued together. The rabbi was dumped onto the floor. He got up and sat in the next one. It broke, too. Right down the line he went, sitting in every chair on display. He sat down good and hard and the chairs went from under him. Harry couldn't believe it. He was still standing by the couch in a pool of sawdust trying to recover his voice, "Wha . . . ? Wha . . . ?"

A crash at the other end of the furniture department where the rabbi had just tried to open the bottom drawer of the black couple's colonial maple bureau (its Masonite frame collapsed) woke Harry up. "What's what?" he shouted at Lux, who in company with the young bridegroom and his wife was surrounded by all the other shoppers in Hot Shot's. What was up? To Harry's and his salesmen's consternation, Rabbi Lux was passing into the store's appliance department.

Too late! Too late! Harry reached the appliance section a second after Rabbi Lux had opened the door of the deluxe model Freezedaire refrigerator with 18 cubic feet of deep-freeze cold—a blast of hot from the open box. "Defrosting!" cried Harry. But the rabbi was scratching the baked-enamel finish and it was peeling off like Scotch tape. "Leave it alone!" screamed Harry, knocking the door shut. As it snapped back in place, it fell off its hinges and smashed to the floor, where the plastic underneath shattered into a thousand pieces.

The rabbi, the couple, and the rest of the shoppers were heading toward the door as Harry called—"I got an A-1 store here. Nothing but the best! Genuine!" he shrieked, banging on a dining-room table. It collapsed. But it was genuine. Solid oak. It broke his foot.

"A hundred thousand!" cried Harry, limping into the center of the board of Beth Rachmoniss, gathered in Yehoodi's Pool Room. "All over Dorchester, Roxbury, Rosindale, even out in Quincy, I got a bad name. For two weeks not a *shvartzer* in the store. And a week I'm in the hospital. What's what?" He pointed to Lefkowitz, secretary of the Beth Rachmoniss board, a man who had sat in federal jail for income-tax evasion, a man known in Beth Rachmoniss for his brains. "You got sense, Lefkowitz, lock him up!"

To lock a man up, however, you got to have an official meeting. The president has to be there.

Where was the president? Still in the hospital.

So in the back room of Yehoodi's, the board of Beth Rachmoniss decided to send its secretary, Lefkowitz, to talk with the president. Everyone respected him in Yehoodi's. Income-tax evasion. An intellectual crime! And Lefkowitz had managed to salt some of his evasion away. In his old age he became penitent and joined the synagogue. Perhaps Rabbi Lux's plea for his release before the parole board had touched his heart. Lefkowitz himself wanted to believe it.

Now Lefkowitz was sent to the hospital to talk.

What happened? Lefkowitz arrived. He sent his name into the president. And the president sent back word that he was having an enema. For two days Lefkowitz waited. After 48 hours, Lefkowitz realized who was getting an enema. It was full of hot air. He left the hospital and went back to report.

Yehoodi's Pool Room and Taxi Stand was in an uproar. No one even noticed Lefkowitz come in the door. Everyone was talking at once and Cockeyed Zitzz was talking loudest of all.

It had happened to him. What were they going to do, Zitzz wanted to know. "Huh?"

The stocky little bookie shook, a featherweight contender. His hands clenched in fists hammered on the pool table. "I'll kill him!" he shouted. "All right!" "I'll hire them from East Boston. Right behind the ear with a .44—on Blue Hill Avenue, they'll do it. Okay!

"Who told him to, huh?" he cried, looking around at the other bookies in the room. "I'll kill *him* and I'll kill you!" And it went on, until one of the big bookies, a cultured man from Newton, stopped him. . . .

The day before, Rabbi Lux had stepped into Cockeyed Zitzz's Egg Store. Zitzz ran the egg store as a front for the business in his back room. Strictly, he was not a horse bookie like Menshevick, but a numbers man. Every day the *Boston Daily Record* printed the

Treasury balance and all over Boston people bet on what the last three numbers would be.

Fifty cents a bet—everyone could afford it, and if you won—500 dollars. Day in and day out men and women, children and adults streamed into the cigar stores, the groceries, the fruit stands and the locksmiths of Boston to place bets. The poorer the section, the more lucrative the numbers. The hope of the 500-dollar prize sustained many a family. So Dorchester was rich pickings for the numbers men and Cockeyed Zitzz's Egg Store on Blue Hill Avenue in the midst of the poor of our community, a silver mine.

The day before, Rabbi Lux had walked in on it. In his black coat he stepped through the door of the egg store. Right up to the counter. Cockeyed came running out of his back room. He asked, "Can I help?"

The rabbi looked at him. He looked at him and tears came into his eyes. He said in a voice of such sadness that it made Zitzz shiver, a voice of trouble and woe, "You got your eggs in the wrong basket." *Vey ist mir!* Zitzz got frightened. His eyes crossed with excitement. The rabbi walked over to the window where the fresh eggs were displayed. He picked a grade A large one up and said, "You don't know up from down. Right from wrong."

It was bad enough scaring Zitzz that way with his own eggs. But then the rabbi stood there, right in the front window, holding up the grade A large. It frightened the customers away. Who wants to place a bet with the rabbi standing like that in the window?

Rabbi Lux had caught Cockeyed right in the middle of the afternoon rush. Customers began to gather outside the store. Nobody would go in—but everybody was anxious to see what the rabbi was up to. A crowd pushed up against the glass window. A hundred mouths going at once. You couldn't hear yourself talk, there was so much noise. Everybody had an idea—what the rabbi was doing.

"Making an omelette!"

"Teaching a lesson!"

"Juggling!"

"Doing a trick! Making a spell . . . you know . . . the magic."

The crowd grew more and more excited, larger and larger. Traffic was held up. The mob had spilled off the sidewalk into Blue Hill Avenue. In the background you could hear a police siren. Station Nine was sending down a patrol car to break up the jam. Fire engines, too! There was so much noise, someone had turned in an alarm.

Nu! Cockeyed Zitzz got scared. Police mean trouble. The fire department chops up your store, fire or not. His eyes, already crossed, began to twitch. The rabbi had been standing in his store for 20 minutes.

Rabbi Lux looked into the window. A hundred noses pushed up against the glass. Runny noses and dry ones. A hundred curious faces were jammed onto the transparent surface. New heads pushed away old ones. Avarice, idiocy, stupidity, senility bloated on the moist glass. Before the rabbi, Dorchester spread out. And then, in the corner of the window, he saw two or three deep wrinkles matted by a wiry gray beard. An old man stared at Rabbi Lux. Fastened on him, bitter and stern. The anger that had impelled him into Zitzz's store ebbed away. "Who can bring a clean thing out of an unclean?"

Rabbi Lux knew the answer. The old man's mouth opened. "Not one," echoed in the toothless hole. The egg shook in the rabbi's hand. He closed his eyes and when he looked up, a little boy was staring at him in the old man's place.

The fire engines were screaming. The police car was right outside. Cockeyed Zitzz was going crazy. He ran up to Lux in the window. "What are you doing, Rabbi?" he sputtered. "Laying an egg?"

The rabbi turned and pointed to the back room.

"You can't go in!" cried Cockeyed. "Private!"

The rabbi raised his finger before Zitzz. He turned again and walked slowly toward the doorway. There he threw open the door and cried out to the crowd—"A Chayrim!"

A Chayrim! The word went through the mob on Blue Hill Avenue as fast as the news of a winning number. Like a flame through cellophane. Rabbi Lux had put a rabbinical ban on Cockeyed Zitzz's establishment.

A hush fell over the street. Even the fire siren died down. "A Chayrim!" exclaimed the rabbi a second time, pointing through the doorway to the back room. Then he strode away, the crowd parting before him as he made his way down Woodrow Avenue.

Cockeyed Zitzz stuck his head out the door of the store. "Business as usual!" he shouted jauntily.

Not one of that huge crowd of customers stirred. Not even the cops would come in to place a number. There was a curse on the egg store.

The odds in the numbers racket are tough enough. A curse in addition! The trade avoided Cockeyed Zitzz's store and went instead to the fruit stand, the shoe shine shop and the bowling alley to place their bets. Zitzz had to conduct business that afternoon in the back seats of the synagogue. No one would go into the egg store. Not even to buy eggs.

At first the other bookies smiled. They had a good laugh behind Cockeyed's back. But when the rabbi started showing up in their places—the smiles disappeared. He was laying on the Chayrim everywhere. The synagogue was becoming the only place to do business. And it wasn't just the bookies who were suffering. Everyone in Dorchester it seemed had a finger in something shady. This one had a colored mistress, that one typed the wrong way on an adding machine. Embezzlement, adultery, fraud, nothing serious, but still such things publicized? It was a shameful business to drag it into the open. There is a Talmudic dictum, if a man finds his evil urge overpowering him, he should go and do his evil in private. Rabbi Illia adds, "Let him act as his passion requires but let him not profane the Name of God in public."

Dorchester kept quiet about its bookies, its murders, its robberies. A decorous community. And here was Rabbi Lux going around, stamping a man's crime on his forehead. The Jews would get a bad name in Massachusetts. Shhh . . . Shhh . . . Rabbi Lux. Don't make a shame of yourself. Shhh . . .

In Yehoodi's Taxi Stand the children of Israel got together, the board of Beth Rachmoniss, and half of Dorchester, to discuss—how to shut Lux up. But the rabbi forestalled them. He had closed Zitzz's Egg Store on a Monday. On the following Saturday matters came to a head. The whole community was buzzing. And Simcha Tantzenn decided to go to *shul*. . . .

CHAPTER THIRTEEN

SIMCHA

SIMCHA TANTZENN. There was a name to dance to. And everyone in Dorchester danced to it—though Simcha did a crooked step.

Simcha was our state senator. Ours? Well, he was Dorchester's. I didn't vote for him. But the Jews did. So did the colored in Roxbury and the Irish in Mattapan. Who thought they could be so stupid?

Simcha was sharp—that was known all over Boston. He had sold the jailhouse three times and the John Hancock Building twice. Simcha who never had a dime! And watch out! Because now I hear he's peddling shares in the Prudential. A check bouncer! A liar! Our Simcha—God love him! And Dorchester's favorite son.

Simcha was lately in high spirits. He had just become a state senator. Dorchester's old one, an attorney, had just been booted up to judge. And Simcha, with the help of the bookies and undertakers in the community, had succeeded him. Simcha could never become a judge. Not that he wasn't intimate with the law, having been hauled into court continually by angry constituents. But he wasn't a lawyer. As he himself advertised, he didn't even have a high-school degree.

Why did he advertise this?

You see, Simcha appealed to the sympathy vote. Give me the job, he told Dorchester. Otherwise I'll starve.

And it was true. There was nothing else Simcha Tantzenn could do. He couldn't add sufficiently to be a bookie. If you don't keep your books, the big boys in Newton get after you. So they sent him to the State House to handle million-dollar budgets. That's how Dorchester thought. Keep Simcha off the streets. Put him in the State House.

"My Heart's in Dorchester," Simcha's posters announced. And Dorchester was flattered. Who else would have the nerve to say such a thing? Everybody in Dorchester wanted to get out of there.

Dorchester knew that Simcha was a sharper, an ignoramus, a faker and a . . . But there was one thing about Simcha that they loved. He was a promiser. He would promise you anything. Really! Anything you wanted. From the Empire State Building to a seat right next to the Messiah on the Day of Judgment. And don't think in Dorchester there weren't requests for such.

In Dorchester—better a promise than nothing. People were even willing to pay for them. And Tantzenn would take your money, with a smile.

Simcha Tantzenn knew how to collect. He had served his political apprenticeship under Mayor Curley of jailhouse fame. Curley's stooge in the Jewish district, after the mayor's demise in city politics, Simcha blossomed into a power in his own right. A heavy man, his weight girdled into a shiny blue-serge suit, Tantzenn made the rounds in Dorchester collecting money, pledges, political power—allying himself with everything cheap, rotten or desperate.

Simcha greeted you with a grin. He waddled forward like a lugubrious penguin, shook your hand daintily, and said, beaming, "God wove you!" Simcha's smile was something. It bordered on the lewd. The fat folds of his cheeks overlapped each other in the fullness of that smile. Such a smile urged you to come out with a proposition, to ask a favor, to let him do something for you.

From table to table he went in the delicatessens of Dorchester, greeting everyone in sight, "Hellow," he lisped, bending over a table. "How are you, God wove you? How are things?" Three times a day he made the rounds of the delicatessens, no matter what business was going on at the State House. Whether Simcha knew you or not, you always got the big hello from him. His nose would quiver over you, sniffing for a promise you might pay for. It was his business.

Now and then he made a mistake. For instance, the time after the great hurricane which knocked down the huge elm trees along Blue Hill Avenue. Electricity all over Dorchester was out. It was just before the elections. Simcha toured Dorchester with a sound truck announcing that he had spoken with the Edison Company and the lights would be on the next day. "I pwomise!" shouted Tantzenn with a joyful lisp. So none of the merchants bought ice for their deep freezers. Five days later, when Edison finally turned the electricity on, thousands and thousands of frozen foods were ruined. And so was Simcha—temporarily.

Why only temporarily? Well, the middle class was deserting Dorchester in a steady stream. Those who were stranded behind needed promises. You can't ruin a merchant in promises. Not a Simcha. Temporarily—

yes. After his defeat at the polls, he deserted his wife, ten children—and ran off to Florida, the race track. But Dorchester called him back. Come back and promise! Back came Simcha, a little seedy and run down, but refreshed in spirit, to take office and dispense promises.

The bookies liked him. So did the crooks, the gamblers, and the undertakers. Here was a man who could be depended on. He would sell his vote in the legislature to the highest bidder. Simcha Tantzenn, when you came right down to it, was a straightforward proposition. On Beacon Hill here was a man you could trust. Simcha was one of them, their boy. With no compunctions they underwrote his campaigns.

And there were some who genuinely liked Simcha. You had to admit—there was something of the artist in him. Something he had either inherited from Mayor Curley or from some ancestor, some *tzaddik* in Galicia, a peddler in miracles. Who else could get the governor to pick up a rubber check? Especially when you drop it in the state treasurer's office. To get an Irish Pol to pick up your tab? In Boston—it was a miracle.

Maybe it was his fake heart attacks that won the heart of Dorchester. Simcha loved attention. He first tried out his act on the floor of the legislature. That's a rough place for beginners. The reps knew he was faking and stoned him with law books. Have you ever picked up the *Legislative Acts of Massachusetts?* A good book, it weighs at least 30 pounds and is a foot and a half thick. A hard black binding. A regular cement block. Simcha collapsed in the aisle, shouting, "Heart! Heart! Heart!"

The books flew through the air. When they dug Simcha out—he went to the hospital in earnest.

His next try, he chose a better place to open. The

Democratic state convention. There are a lot of amateurs from the west and south of the state. What do they know about Simcha Tantzenn?

Nobody was paying Simcha any attention that day. His vote had already been bought. So suddenly Simcha jumps up, grabs the microphone in the Dorchester section and shouts over the loudspeaker system, "Heart! Heart! Ayyyyyyyy!" And he collapses. He takes a real dive. Because he's standing on his henchman, Cockeyed Zitzz's head. The boys from Dorchester and South Boston laugh and hiss. But from Worchester and Framingham and Springfield goes up a moan and a groan. "Ambulance! Ambulance!" A siren starts up. The cops clear the aisles. They take Simcha down the main aisle on a stretcher with the band from Peabody playing a funeral march. It was impressive. It stopped the convention. It got in all four Boston newspapers. Simcha Tantzenn was known all over the state.

But the coup d'état was the St. Patrick's Day parade. Simcha was running for mayor. It was a joke. He wouldn't get enough votes to qualify. A *pish* in the bucket he would get. But he would get attention. Simcha announced his candidacy early. Early enough to get a place of honor in the St. Patrick's Day parade. The Irish told him to stick his finger in his *tochis*. He could ride with the sanitation department. In the back of a truck. They had enough Irish Simcha Tantzenns. They didn't need a Jewish one on parade.

So Simcha, that genius of political tactic, our Simcha, hired a jeep. He got out his best tuxedo, dressed Cockeyed Zitzz up in a military uniform and got one of the queers from downtown Boston to drive. Cockeyed Zitzz is dressed in what looks like a full colonel's uniform. And the queer is dressed like a private. Their insignia is strange. But on St. Patrick's Day nobody is going to notice the difference. Not in South Boston, where they have been drinking Jack Daniels by the bottle since four in the morning. The parade starts. The bands begin. And unobtrusively, right in back of the governor's limousine, the open one, bearing the most important politicians in the parade, a jeep wheels out from a side street and, cutting in front of the honor guard, begins to follow.

Guess who? Cockeyed Zitzz is standing up, in a bird colonel's uniform, saluting Simcha. And Simcha is waving to the crowd, to the honor guard, to the limousine with the biggest Pols in Boston in it. "God wwhhovvve you!" Simcha cries out as loud as he can. "God wwhhovvve you!"

If that had been the end of it. Listen, the Pols can take a joke. It would have meant stopping the parade and getting a Sherman tank to dislodge Simcha from his position. "Let him have a little fun," said the governor. "What the hell." Let him get a hand in South Boston. What good would it do him?

And then, right in front of the grand reviewing stand, right in front of the huge platform hung with red, white and green bunting; where the lord mayor of Dublin is standing, with his long *shillelagh,* looking at the great sight of the whole of the Boston Irish strung out for miles in every direction; where the crowd is thickest and the brass is shiniest; Simcha Tantzenn picks up a military loudspeaker and yells, "Heart! Heart!"

Oy vey! Catastrophe. Cockeyed Zitzz catches Simcha as he falls. The queer runs the jeep into the reviewing stand. The ambulance starts screaming. The parade jams and grinds to a stop. The band on the stand starts to play, to cover it all. The honor guard lowers its bayonets. All over Boston noontime whistles shriek. And nobody has told the lord mayor about Simcha

Tantzenn. Gathering the skirts of his robes, he has hurried down the steps of the stand. Looking over the stricken politician, he orders the cops to lift him up to the stand. So they carry Simcha to the place of honor, right next to the microphone. Simcha revives. The lord mayor whispers, "Praise God!" And it carries into the mike. Down the length of South Boston it echoes, "Praise God!" in a thick Irish brogue. Well—the cheers are deafening. And Simcha, taking hold of the lord mayor's shillelagh, raises himself up and whispers into the mike to a million Irishmen—"God wwhhovve you."

What can I say? It was a historic moment. Not only did all the papers in New England cover it, but it was on a national television hook-up. Simcha Tantzenn had stolen the St. Patrick's Day parade. He came close to being mayor.

So it was no mean adversary that was going to synagogue to see what Rabbi Lux was doing. Simcha might be a fool—but dangerous.

Needless to say, there was a big turnout at *shul* that Sabbath. There was an edge of expectancy in the air. Two women were absent. One was Mrs. Blatz, who hadn't come since her Harvey had disappeared. The other was Yehoodiss Lux. For several weeks now the rabbi's wife had not been showing up at services. Everyone else, however, was there.

CHAPTER FOURTEEN

HORSES AND CHARIOTS

THE WORD had spread. Something was up. All of Dorchester was there. From Roxbury they came even, the handful of old beards that were left. And the agnostics of Mattapan showed up. The shoeshine boys, the plumbers, the bakers, the painters, the upholsterers, the dry-cleaning people, the aged and infirm from the housing projects, a teenage gang from the Hecht House and every taxi driver in the district. There was even a group from the state mental hospital. Word had gotten behind the walls, and the patients started clamoring to go to *shul.*

Beth Rachmoniss was packed. You couldn't get a seat on the windowsills. There was a crowd backing out of the entrance on the side of the hall and down the stairways into the street. Everybody whispering, pinching his neighbor, making fun under his breath. They only filled the place like this on the Day of Atonement. And there was the same feeling in the air—good and evil were about to clash. Only instead of the ram's horn blowing, it would be Rabbi Lux. The crowd rubbed its hands with joy. The bookies were pushing their way though the mob to their seats in the back of the synagogue.

Dressed in conservative black banking suits (the business image), Dorchester's bookies shoved their way in. Twelve of them led by Menshivick, the white-haired brains of Blue Hill Avenue's no-goodniks. The service had been going on a while when they arrived. Cockeyed Zitzz was already there. He had kept a pew empty for his friends and done a little business on the side. Bustling down the aisle now, Zitzz greeted the boys with nervous effusion. "This way! This way!" he shouts over the drone of the congregation and the voice of the cantor. Everybody, of course, looks around. They begin to buzz. And Cockeyed, brimming with self-importance, leads the bookies to their seats.

A little trouble! Several old men had settled in the bookies' pew as Zitzz went up the aisle to greet the gangsters. After all, the *shul* is crowded. Who has a right to hold seats? The old beards have to be evicted now. There is noise—an outcry. They're not moving. A fist is raised. A bookie is kicked. Someone almost pulls a gun. The whole *shul* begins to shout . . . "Shah!" "Still!" "Shame!" "Quiet!" "A shande!" "A shande!" Cockeyed Zitzz is cracked on the back of the head with a prayer book. Threats! Filthy language! A fist fight!

Just at this moment who should enter? It was arranged at Yehoodi's. A moment after the bookies, he started through the crowd. The queer from Stuart Street is at his side. Simcha Tantzenn! All smiles. Shaking hands with everybody. It takes him ten minutes to get up the stairs, he's saying hello to so many people.

A song and dance on the stairs! Simcha ladles out promises like oil among the excited throng. Right and left he gives away assurances.

"Didn't I pwomithe?" "It's yourth." "I'll take care of it." "Don't wowwy—the firth thing." "You bet." "I'm with you." "Twutht me." "A 100 perthent" "In your handth—tomowwow."

Oh, Solomon—you yourself couldn't make good on the favors that Simcha promised in the space of one minute on those stairs. This one he would get into public housing . . . that had been closed for three years. That one he would get a position in the governor's office. A third one was assured his son would enter Harvard in the spring. Simcha would talk to the overseers. Listen—he was going to see the President personally to get a special poverty program for Dorchester.

"Isn't the Blue Hill an Appalachian?" shouted someone.

"Wight," said Simcha, bending toward the ear of the idiot who had just spoken. "Keep it under your hat. You firtht."

To the toothless he whispered, "I'll get you teeth." For the eyeless there would be eyes. For the deaf, new hearing aids. Simcha pinched the steel shank of an amputee. "You'll walk again." He beamed at the invalid. "A special operation, I'll see to it—don't wowwy."

The mob of frantic constituents engulfed Simcha as he climbed the steps of Beth Rachmoniss to the hall upstairs. Everyone was eager to say hello, to slip a five-dollar bill into his fingers. The small change was falling out of Simcha's pockets.

He reached the door just as a fight was about to erupt inside. Cockeyed Zitzz had pulled a blackjack. The *shul* was in an uproar. Simcha saved the situation. Standing in the open doorway, he doffed his homburg gaily, to show an orange and pink yarmulkah, sprinkled with golden stars. And the queer takes off his beanie. He's got a green yarmulkah with a big shamrock on it.

The crowd on the stairs begins to laugh. What will Simcha do next? The laughter spreads into the hall and the *shul* quiets down. Tantzenn is here. With an Irish queer—a green yarmulkah no less. From the parade. Everyone chuckles. A showman! People start to sit down. Even Cockeyed Zitzz takes his seat, wedging in beside Menshivick.

So Simcha makes an entrance. He is waving at everybody. He gives a big nod to his pals the bookies. But he doesn't sit with them. No . . . no . . . Tantzenn walks right down the aisle and takes a seat among the pious in the first few rows. Then he turns around and waves to everybody. He and the queer! And a thrill runs through the *shul.*

All eyes turn to the rabbi. But Rabbi Lux sits crumpled like a paper bag in his carved oaken chair. He is wrapped in the large folds of his white and black banded prayer shawl. He huddles like a sick man in his blanket. The rabbi's face is ashen. He sways a little to the sound of the cantor's voice, intoning the prayers, but his lips hardly move. It is the Shabbat Rosh Chodesh—a joyful time—when the New Moon falls on the Sabbath. Yet Rabbi Lux's face was the destruction of the Temple, Tisha B'Ab. He sits downcast in his seat. If he noticed Simcha come in, he gives no sign of it. The whole congregation has their eyes on Rabbi Lux. And all Rabbi Lux does is to hum the cantor's melody dolefully to himself. He picks his nose, hums.

"What's going on?" "Come on!" "Is he a chicken?" An ugly murmuring went through the *shul.* They had come for a show. A throat cutting! A match! Come on, Rabbi!

Come out of the corner! Get up from the chair. Show a little fight. Let's have some excitement. We didn't come to *shul* to pick our noses.

Others in the hall were more compassionate. "Was he afraid?" "He doesn't look so good." Maybe someone had told them a story? The rabbi didn't look like he wanted to pick a fight with anyone. In fact—he seemed so sad, sitting meekly in his large chair, you felt sorry for him. Could he really have done the damage attributed? Many in the *shul* had known Rabbi Lux for years. He had presided over their weddings, Bar Mitzvahs, funerals. . . . And to see him now in such poor health. His black silk yarmulkah, which was squared in the old manner, squatted disconsolately on his head. He swayed in his seat, his eyes wandering aimlessly over the cover of his prayer book. And he had been having troubles lately. His wife wasn't well. Maybe he had gotten a little upset. Was it right to trouble him?

The *shul* began to realize that Rabbi Lux didn't look too well. He had hardly gotten up to conduct the service. The vice-president and the cantor were carrying it on. Hunched over in his seat, the rabbi was shivering in his tallis. A sadness emanated from his chair, filling the hall. The murmuring in the congregation began to quiet down. The tide of ugly talk reversed itself. An unexpected current of pity and even shame began to flow backward through the pews. Shhh . . . Shhh . . . The rabbi is sick . . . Shhhhh . . .

The hush even rippled down among the crowd on the stairs. The noise stopped. Someone started handing prayer books out the door and, abashed, the men and women in the passageway began to turn the pages, the dregs of Dorchester standing on the steps of Beth Rachmoniss and out into the street, their noses in dusty prayer books, stumbling over the unfamiliar Hebrew.

In 20-degree weather, the end of November, it seemed as if Evil and its works were out in the cold. Yet inside the *shul*, on the bema, those who were conducting the service were uneasy. It wasn't the congregation that bothered them. The hall was still. Oil on troubled waters. Imperceptibly, in pew after pew, people had fallen into the rhythm of the service and begun to pray. It was the rabbi. There was something on his face besides sadness. Up close you could see a stubborn muscle pinch his lower lip so it trembled like a hummingbird. You could feel the whole of him trembling under the thin folds of his tallis. The polite questions of the vice-president and the cantor he ignored. Instead, he looked up at them with eyes full of tears. Unnerved, they backed away. The rabbi shook his head and looked down at his black shoes, his breath coming in short, sharp gasps, as if choking. "Eh! Eh!" He bit his lips. The cry was stifled within him. Several times when the cantor was singing, as the chant caught in his throat, the rabbi would half-rise in his seat, swaying on his legs, as he sang to himself, "Eh! Eh!"

Yet the waters of peace slowly rocking the congregation had a soothing effect on the rabbi. His face relaxed. He straightened his prayer shawl. He pressed a fold of it against his damp forehead. Leaning back in his chair, Rabbi Lux sighed. Only his lip continued to tremble, like a stubborn child, a red lip, hot and fitful.

It was during the Eighteen Benedictions. Everyone was quiet. You know how still the *shul* gets when each man has to recite the blessings to himself. Here and there you hear someone singing half-aloud. For the most part people pray under their breath. There's a hush. You can hear a whisper in the hall. For a while you can hear yourself think.

Even a bookie, at such a time, is tempted to look in his prayer book. To think about the God of Abraham,

Isaac and Jacob. To wonder if the verse "Thou Helper, Redeemer, and Shield" could apply.

The hall is quiet—a mumble here and there. The stairs are quiet. Out in the chilly street it's quiet. And the rabbi starts to shake. In the congregation they are nodding over their books. No one notices. Beads of sweat break out on his forehead. He starts to leaf through the pages of his prayer book. Looking up, he shouts, "Menshivick! Turn to page 75."

It rings through the hall. Clear and distinct. Everybody looks up at the rabbi, including the bookie, Menshivick.

"You stupid, Menshivick?" cries the rabbi, even louder. "Page 75! It's for you! 'The horse and his rider hath He thrown into the sea.' Suffolk Downs! You'll lose your pants and you'll be cast in the sea."

The rabbi is standing up on the edge of the bema, shaking, white, a ghost. The congregation begins to murmur. They thumb in confusion through their books. There is the passage on page 75. No one thought of applying it to the race track at Suffolk Downs. And now the rabbi cries out—"Five lines down! יָרְדוּ בִמְצוֹלֹת כְּמוֹ אָבֶן; 'They went down into the depths like a stone.' Like your friend Lipshitz, the Chelsea book. His feet in a tub of cement. To the bottom of Newton reservoir. Your horses will carry you that way. They'll dump you into Boston Bay!"

The rabbi pointed his pale finger to the back of the hall where Menshivick sat. The whole congregation turned around to look at the book. Menshivick, however, was frightened. He knew that his credit was slipping with the big Jew in Newton. New crooks had been coming into Dorchester from the North End. And it's not a pleasant thought—to be sitting in your own tombstone. On the bottom of the ocean—the odds had been pointing in that direction. Now this warning, right from the bema. . . . A violent fear saddled the bookie's mind. His thoughts shied. They galloped in every direction. The reins twisted in his mouth. He couldn't speak.

In that moment Simcha Tantzenn raises his fullness. He gets up with a smile like a mouthful of chicken fat. This is the reason he has come to *shul*. To smooth things over. To make peace among the Jews.

Simcha gathers the crisp folds of his Dacron prayer shawl. Grinning, he begins to squeeze his way out of the crowded pew of the pious, rubbing the old men on their knees, winking at his admirers. "Wabbi!"

"Wabbi!" he calls out again, like you call—wait a second! Simcha is confident. He and the rabbi will settle everything in a shady corner of the ark. He is just pushing out into the aisle . . .

"יַעֲמוֹד Simcha Tantzenn!" Everybody looks around. It is the traditional cry which summons a man to the honor of reading from the holy Torah. But it's not time in the service to read from the Law. And Simcha Tantzenn doesn't know a word of Hebrew.

"יַעֲמוֹד Simcha Tantzenn!" A beautiful tenor voice is calling Simcha to the Torah. Who should it belong to but the rabbi.

Simcha stops. He stands, one foot in the pew, the other in the aisle. He doesn't know that it's not the right time. He does know that he can't read Hebrew. Yet to recite from the Torah. It's an honor. A man can't refuse. You look like an ignoramus. He knows—Dorchester is watching him.

What can he do? Try to mumble through? Simcha beams warmly and gratefully up at Rabbi Lux. Such a smile! Modesty and humility, reticence drip from the corners of the politician's mouth and run in grease stains down his chin. A great honor! Let someone else have it. Simcha goes to sit down. But Rabbi Lux is looking at him. He is imitating the oily smile. He looks Tantzenn right in the eye, giving him his own smile. Lifting that unctuous smile off Simcha's lips, he holds it aloft, showing it to the congregation.

There, on the rabbi's face, the smile goes bad.

The rabbi mocks the whole congregation with a rancid smile. There's a bad odor in the air. People squirm in their seats. But the rabbi keeps smiling. And he begins to croon, clearly and slightly off key, "Simcha . . . Oy Si-i-im-cha . . . Oy Si-i-i-i-i-i-i-mmmmmm chaaaaaaaa . . ."

Simcha gets up again. He starts to waddle down the aisle. He wants to talk to the rabbi. He doesn't think this is in the service.

Rabbi Lux broke off his chant and called to Tantzenn. "אֲרוֹמִמְךָ. Simcha. 'I will extol you, Simcha!' Please turn to page 37. Oy Simcha, 'You brought up my soul from the grave.' Three lines down, everyone! 'His favor is for a lifetime.' "

Simcha stopped in his tracks. The congregation stopped murmuring. The rabbi with a bloodless face looked down at Simcha. He smiled.

"Wabbi . . ." stammered the politician.

The rabbi interrupted him. In a sweet voice he inquired, "Don't your favors last for a lifetime?"

"Of courthe, but I . . ." but Tantzenn didn't get to finish because the rabbi shouts out—"Give unto Simcha, give unto Simcha glory and strength. Give unto Simcha the glory due to his name; take an offering, and come before him."

Dumbfounded, Simcha turned around to a friend in the pew just behind him. As Simcha bent over to check that this was not a customary prayer, the rabbi announced: "How many gave an offering to Simcha on the way in? Will all those please turn to page 67 and recite after me—'Praise ye Simcha; for it is good to sing praises to our Simcha; for it is pleasant and praise is seemly. Simcha doth build up Dorchester. He gathers together the outcasts of Israel. He heals the broken in heart, and binds up their wounds.' Isn't that right?" asked the rabbi. " 'He counts the number of the stars: He calls them all by their names. Great is our Simcha, and mighty in power; His understanding is infinite. . . .' "

"Wabbi!" bellowed Simcha Tantzenn. "What . . . ?"

"Simcha!" the rabbi called back to him. "Come, Simcha! Come on up! Lead the services! Please, Simcha —come up and lead us. Bring your friend, too. Step inside the ark. Right beside the Law. We'll pull the curtain on you. Do whatever you do. Come, Simcha! Come up! Be the rabbi! Please, take a hold in the service."

This wasn't Simcha's kind of game. It was time to go away. Come again another day. Smiling nervously, he backed down the aisle, shaking a few hands and whispering that he was heading for the men's room—an emergency. The rabbi had mistaken his intention. Tantzenn chortled, signaling urgently with his index finger to the queer, Get up and get out.

Too late. As the green skullcap bobbed up and began to jiggle out of the pew of the pious, the rabbi spoke out —"*Nu,* lady? You too! Come on up. Be the cantor. We need a voice like yours. With a green yarmulkah . . ." The rabbi interrupted himself. "Ah . . . you going to the men's room, too?"

A titter ran through the whole hall. "Come on, sing us a song!" the rabbi cried at the flustered couple. "Page 41. 'Sing unto Him, sing praises unto Him.' Come on, everyone, sing!" shouted Rabbi Lux. " 'Tell ye of his marvelous works. Glory ye in his holy name. Search for

Simcha and His strength: seek His face.' Have a good time!" the rabbi cried as the two fled out the door.

"Keep reading!" Lux shouted. "The seed of Israel. His chosen ones. Remember his covenant. He'll give you your inheritance. Right here in Dorchester. It's in another text—'Behold, I will corrupt your seed, and spread dung upon your face.' "

The wasted figure stood on the edge of the bema. "Rosh Chodesh. 'Israel was holiness unto the Eternal and the first fruits of His increase.' "

"Who are you?"

"Who are *you?*" a voice shouted back. It was Menshivick. He had gotten hold of his tongue. The bookies had pushed him to his feet. In a hoarse whinny he shouted back, "I can quote Scripture, too! Take a look—Ecclesiastes: Chapter Seven: Verse 16: 'Be not righteous overmuch; neither make thyself over wise. Why should you destroy yourself?'

"You're a sick man. Don't destroy yourself." From the back of the hall, over the heads of the whole congregation, Menshivick neighed at the rabbi. Rabbi Lux's face was white hot. He trembled like a silken tassel. A thread snapping in the wind. His prayer shawl was soaked in sweat. His cheeks were bright, they gleamed, a hectic light in them. Blood was on the rabbi's lips. But as he opened his mouth, there was a commotion on the stairs.

A rumor, a story, a fact, something was spreading from mouth to mouth in excited talk throughout the hall. Someone whispered it to Cockeyed Zitzz, who jumped up on the seat of his pew and screamed—"Your wife, Lux, *nuts!* She went nuts! They took her to the hospital in the ambulance. Just now!"

The whole synagogue was thrown into confusion. Everyone talking at once. Screaming . . . shouting . . .

Something struck Rabbi Lux, a bolt of electricity. He opened his mouth to cry and his body was jerked. Every feature in his face contorted. With a crash he fell into the first pew.

The *shul* was in an uproar. In the pew, a few helped the rabbi up. Unsteady on his feet, he staggered down the aisle. On all sides babble. "Crazy!" "Nuts!" "I knew she was." "Him, too!" "It runs in the family!" The old men who were propping him up tried to quiet them down. It was no use. Right through the *shul* and down the stairs, Rabbi Lux had to run a gauntlet.

Out on the street he pushed his way through the mob and shook off his comforters. He was all right. He was all right. He was going home. He could do it alone. A little fresh air.

It was freezing cold—they protested, 20 degrees. He was sweating. Pneumonia! But the rabbi broke away. His full banded shawl billowing in the cold wind, he began to run. In his damp black suit he ran down the avenue, rushing toward his home.

CHAPTER FIFTEEN

SEAS

YES, Yehoodiss had been taken to the hospital. It was true. The last few weeks had put a nervous strain on her as well as the rabbi. His strange behavior had not gone unnoticed. Yet it was not certain that she understood it. On account of the telephone calls, Yehoodiss had hardened her heart. No love—no sympathy. Let the rabbi do without it. She would bring him to his knees.

But whose heart was it—that heart? It was no easy task for a woman with a heart as big as Yehoodiss' to harden it; to sit across the table and watch her husband the rabbi starving, sweating, flushed with fever; and to say nothing, do nothing. It gave her a cramp in the chest. Her face was impassive but her heart was turning over. The arteries, the glands, the organs that pumped up sympathy, all had to reabsorb their produce as gall and bile. Yehoodiss began to suffer. And she refused to show it. She scowled and fought back tears. No hysteria. No nothing. She sat at the table, silently, and refused to answer any of her husband's questions. The rabbi could talk to Mrs. Blatz if he wanted to. She had her own business.

So the rabbi got up, saddened by his wife's intransigence. "Please! Please!" she wanted to cry. But she twisted her lips in. Paler and even more feverish, the rabbi left the house.

Yehoodiss would jump up and begin to slice carrots or cucumbers. Wielding a big butcher knife! Dozens of them she would slice until a carnage of vegetables lying in their own juices covered the table. Furiously she scraped them off the tabletop with the knife into an open paper bag, which she dumped in the garbage pail. Shouting and crying, she would begin to chop again until the table was covered or the telephone rang.

Oh yes, the telephone still rang for Yehoodiss. But now the stories coming back were about the rabbi. And Yehoodiss didn't want to hear. "Talk to me about something else!" she demanded. When her friends complained this was the thing Dorchester was talking about, Yehoodiss slammed the receiver against the wall. She lost her correspondents.

The mornings and afternoons became lonelier. She refused to go to *shul.* Most of the day she wandered through her house with a broom, wiping away imaginary spider webs, mumbling to herself. Her large breasts were swollen. She cried from the pain. And in her head there was a continual buzzing like a telephone busy signal.

Buizzzzzy! Buizzzzzzt! Buizzzzzy! Buizzzzzzt!

"Stop it!" she shouted, holding her head. "Stop it! Stop it!"

Several times the neighbors came upstairs and knocked on the door to ask what was wrong.

"Nothing, nothing . . ." Yehoodiss insisted from behind a closed door. She was in tears. "Cramps! Cramps!"

Aimlessly the rabbi's wife made her way through the four rooms of her dingy apartment. In the front parlor there was a balding carpet. The overstuffed couch and the sitting chair with a broken spring were upholstered in a faded cherry velvet. The furniture was all inherited from the rabbi's parents. Ugly and out of fashion, it made Yehoodiss unhappy when she sat there.

The bedroom was also furnished with the property of Rabbi Lux's ancestors. Two enormous but lumpy beds, set in unshakable carved oak frames, had been brought over the Atlantic. They crowded out the possibility of any other furniture in the bedroom. One companion had been jammed into the room. This was an oak bureau, chipped, with drawers that stuck and a faint smell of herring clinging to the bottom half. Only the yellow rayon curtains in the bedroom were Yehoodiss' doing. And they got dirty too quickly. It was not a congenial room.

The rabbi's study, its musty books and hard chairs cushioned in cracked black leather—this was not a place for a feminine heart. So the kitchen and the toilet remained.

It was in the kitchen that Yehoodiss had sat most frequently, a bright-flowered print of red and blue teacups on the walls. The table with chrome legs and a white plastic top that she had installed, throwing out the old one, this was her altar. Here she could bang her head and feel at home. She was surrounded by her things. The refrigerator wheezed. A tea kettle boiled on the stove. And the phone might ring any minute.

Since Mrs. Blatz's calls, the bright walls of the kitchen had been haunted. Yehoodiss lay in bed for hours nursing a headache. Or she leafed through books she wasn't interested in, sitting in the rabbi's study. For a while she pretended to knit, in the front parlor.

As the buzzing in her head grew louder, Yehoodiss could not sit. Nervously she paced through the rooms of the apartment, doing her household tasks with a blind, tremulous energy. She would wash the same dish for an hour, standing over the bubbling sink, her thoughts wandering off. She scrubbed and scrubbed, her hands red and raw, the water running hotter and hotter, the immaculate plate turning and turning in her hands.

Who was she? This woman. This Mrs. Blatz. A widow —eh? No—a divorcee. She lost her husband—a runaway. The son, too. She's on the lookout!

In the little passageway between the kitchen and the bedroom Yehoodiss stood with a broom, sweeping the same spot on the stained green linoleum, over and over.

Where's Harvey—eh? She doesn't know? She's not looking for Harvey. A man—that's what she's got an eye out for. Running up and down the street—with a weapon! Hot pants is what she's got, this Mrs. Blatz. Who gave her the rabbi's number? Someone in the sisterhood?

Seated on the edge of the double bed, Yehoodiss stared angrily through the window hung with yellow rayon curtains. She hadn't cleaned them in a while. They were dirty. So was the sock in her hand. It had a large hole in its heel. Yehoodiss was darning it. Back and forth the needle went through the same hole as the minutes lengthened into hours.

This Harvey. He was around somewhere. A little pest. Hiding like he used to. The rabbi was late for supper more than once for Harvey Blatz's sake. Yehoodiss saw a small boy with pimples on his face, dressed in a shiny blue suit, standing in an alley. He was whistling suggestively through skinny fingers. Rabbi Lux was passing by. The boy winked and crooked his finger, enticing the rabbi into the alley. There, behind the garbage cans, lurked Mrs. Blatz in a silk negligee. She picked up her white slip and showed her large and milky thighs. Her yellow rayon bloomers. Higher and higher she raised up her slip before the rabbi's eyes. Harvey stood behind her, shaking her buttocks.

Oy—the needle stuck in Yehoodiss' thumb. It began to bleed over her hands.

A whore! A whore! Yehoodiss wound the sock around her thumb. Running out into the hall, she grabbed the broom and came back into the bedroom, smashing it through the window. The jagged edges glinted in the frame. The broom was entangled with yellow rayon streamers as Yehoodiss hacked at the jutting fragments with the wooden handle. "Whore! Whore!" she shouted. She wanted to put her own fist through the glass.

The delinquents had done it, with stones, Yehoodiss explained, tersely, to the rabbi that night. Inside her, however, windows were still being shattered. And stones were being piled on her heart. When the rabbi left the next morning, she began to chop cucumbers furiously.

Something was going on. Of that she was certain. The rabbi was coming home spent and feverish. What did it mean? At night he lay on the other side of the bed. No energy.

Nu! They were doing it. The phone calls hadn't been so frequent lately. They were meeting somewhere, the two of them. And that Harvey! At the table the other night, the rabbi had been sweating. Breathing hard. All right! She wouldn't say anything. All right! Let them! Slamming down the butcher knife, Yehoodiss narrowly missed chopping off her thumb.

She grabbed a handful of the dismembered vegetables, dropped them into a pot on the kitchen stove and let them boil.

So—a divorce. She'd let him have a divorce. That was it! No—she wouldn't. Let him beg and cry. Let the fat Mrs. Blatz come crawling up the stairs, step by step. She would kick her down and let her beg for forgiveness. Let the two of them hold hands at the bottom of the stairs and beg. From three flights up—she would spit on them.

Tssssssspppppp! And the pot boiled over and onto the floor. A long trail of tiny bubbles in a lacy veil hissed on the linoleum.

Garbage! She would throw garbage at them! Let them stink under it. *Nu!* At the bottom of three flights. Yehoodiss was standing by the toilet, where she had gone to get a mop. She was pulling the chain up and down. The water cabinet was bone dry and the apparatus only made a dry, rushing sound. "No divorce! No divorce!"

"You hear! Hear! No divorce! Hang on me! Weep on me! No divorce. No separation." Yehoodiss was standing over her plastic table. It was Saturday. The buzzing in her head was driving her crazy. She emptied the whole fruit and vegetable bin onto the white top. She was quivering. The phone rang. She hurled a grapefruit at the receiver. "Never! Never!" she shouted at the black box. Grabbing a butcher knife, she began to scream. No! No! No! She'd cut her wrists first.

It was an accident. "Accident! Accident!" Yehoodiss screamed as the blood spurted out. A dark red line twisted back and forth across the tabletop, running in streams through the clotted mass of vegetables and fruits, running with their juices off the white plastic onto the floor.

"Accident! Accident!" Yehoodiss called out, hysterical. It took the neighbors a while to respond. They had come before for nothing. The ones directly below her were at services that morning in Beth Rachmoniss. In fact, it was a telephone repairman who found her. The phone had been off the hook for an hour.

CHAPTER SIXTEEN

ROCK BOTTOM

ALONG Blue Hill Avenue came Rabbi Lux running, tripping in his long black and white shawl. He was a man sprung from a steam box and plunged into ice. The fever was broken. His anger fled down the avenue before him. He shivered in the freezing winds. The heat that had racked his bones for weeks was gone. In its place, fear made the limbs of Rabbi Lux tremble with cold. Yehoodiss! He was terrified. Yehoodiss? What had he done?

He had killed her. A woman of feeling, his wife . . . not the kind to play games with. And he had been stubborn, proud. He had irritated her. He knew it. He *had* known it. His meekness made her angry. And he had continued to be meek. But insisting on his way.

Oh yes, insisting on his way. What was he—the Master of Righteousness? He could have hung up on this Mrs. Blatz. It wasn't right? So what! David had bowed before Bathsheba. He could have bent a little before Yehoodiss. Why hadn't he hung up? His wife! His wife! He had never appreciated her. She loved him. How many men are blessed to receive such a love? A little-hearted pig he had been. Stubborn in his way.

A pig! A pig! Rabbi Lux named himself. As a pig he had sat in judgment on the world. A pig in a rabbi's clothing. All these weeks he had sat across the table from his wife, feeding on his pride. Nourishing himself on humility. A word would have stopped it. "Shhhhhh . . . Shhhhhh . . ." A ridiculous sound! And how many people had he said it to? How stubbornly he had refused to listen. Even when they barked.

The idea of his stubbornness took hold of Rabbi Lux. It filled him with amazement. It rose with the icy drafts from the street, under his garments. His legs, chapped, stung. His head smarted. All these years he had withheld himself. His finger was in his ear. His hand before his eyes. A pious nincompoop! He had refused to understand.

What had happened at home? His wife had been angry. That was the situation—he didn't see it? Avoid anger. Don't recognize. Why? He could have called to it. He could even have shouted at it. He could have gotten angry himself. After all, he was only human. Even God got angry. If the world is outrageous to God, should it be good to Rabbi Lux? He loses his temper and you smile. "Behold he putteth no trust in his saints." Why should He? They don't see what's in front of their noses. Justice? A WORD. Experience makes fun of it. And what do His saints do? They turn their heads away. They smile on life. They ignore it. Everywhere, as is written, men eat the flesh of their own arms. They take a bite out of each other. What do His saints do? They go about nodding with closed eyes. In secluded places they recline, where the noise of the world won't reach them. There they judge. And they judge without anger.

What does it mean? What? Two thousand years ago the famous school of Shammai insisted—better if God had never created the world! With sticks and stones maintained it against the school of Hillel, pleading—better that God created the world. Hillel's students were locked out of the schoolhouse. Beaten up in the streets. For 20 years the optimists pleaded. In that time they must have learned something. They compromised. The world was a botch, but—look to your deeds.

His deeds. How many troubles had people brought to him? And he sent them home with a nice smile, a sweet word. Wrong! Wrong! You should have sent them home with gall and wormwood. It was ridiculous! Why should man suffer? An indignity! He should have ripped their clothes and sent them home in mourning. For life. Let men know—it's crazy.

"*Nu!*" "*Nu,* Rabbi!" "You heard!" A group of Rabbi Lux's neighbors were gathered on the front porch of his house. They saw him coming down Blue Hill Avenue toward them and called out. Despite the cold, the excitement of the ambulance just a little while before had brought them. They had carried Yehoodiss out in a yellow bathrobe caked with crimson. And now the neighbors, stamping their feet to keep warm, were waiting anxiously for the rabbi to come along. They were mostly old people who couldn't make it to *shul* on such a cold day. For the ambulance they had come out, and now they stayed out, waiting for the rabbi.

He ran up onto the porch. "What happened?" he asked.

"Blood!" "All over." "A mess." "Right on the stairs." "On the sidewalk."

"How b . . . bad?" stammered Rabbi Lux.

Nobody knew. They all looked at each other. The only question anyone had asked the ambulance people was—what happened? Finally one of the neighbors piped up in a cracked voice, "Crazy!" It was an old man of ninety who lived next door. He limped up to the rabbi, his beard yellowed with tobacco spittle, and opening his palms explained apologetically in falsetto, "Crazy, that's all they said."

"Where did they take her? Can you tell me?" begged Rabbi Lux. Nobody knew for sure. The hospital, the morgue, the crazy house—there were a dozen suggestions. After a minute of this, the rabbi, getting sick, elbowed his way through the small, excited circle of neighbors on the porch. Opening the door, he went up the stairs, climbing hastily to his apartment. Maybe the ambulance people had left a note there. His fingers shook as he unlocked the door. His heart was fumbling too, beating wildly in his chest.

Walking into the kitchen, he saw blood on the table. The floor was still wet. The gore floated among the vegetable juices. The room began to tip in the rabbi's sight and he felt himself slipping. Dizzy, he leaned against the wall and tried to focus on the table, searching for a note. A fly hovered in the air. It flew up from the sticky refuse on the floor and began to buzz in the rabbi's ear. He tried to brush it away.

Ding . . . ding . . . ding . . . dong.

The phone was ringing. Maybe it was the hospital? His hand trembling, the rabbi lifted the receiver off its hook.

"Hello, is Harvey there?"

"No," said Rabbi Lux.

"Where is he?" the voice demanded angrily.

"Mrs. Blatz," said Rabbi Lux. He tried to breathe. "Mrs. Blatz, listen. Your Harvey isn't here. Please, I can't talk. I'm expecting a call."

"Where?" the voice reiterated.

"Mrs. Blatz, please. Don't do this. I beg you."

"You got to tell me!" the voice insisted.

"Stop it!" exclaimed the rabbi.

"Tell me! Just tell me!" shouted the voice.

"I'll tell you. I'll tell you!" shouted the rabbi back, in a tremulous voice. "You want to know! All right. You want to know? Harvey is dead. You hear, Mrs. Blatz? I can't help it. You can't help it. What can we do? He's not alive."

There was silence on the other end. The rabbi said softly, "What can we do? I'm sorry." He began to cry. "Your Harvey was my student. Is my flesh of brass? I didn't want to tell you. I didn't want him to die. Please. Please. Believe me. Why should he die? Why?"

Tears ran down the rabbi's cheeks. "Why should he die, Mrs. Blatz? He wasn't a bad boy. He made a few mistakes in school. He ran away from home. For that they should murder him? Mrs. Blatz, you loved him. You couldn't get enough. A wedge of gold—your boy. You waited outside every day to take him home from school. Your little one. Your only thing. Why? I want to know why was he taken from you?

"Oy, Harvey!" wailed Rabbi Lux. "My Harvey! My Harvey! What did they do to you?" He was weeping hysterically into the phone. "Let him go! Let him go!" A whole universe that had been locked in the rabbi's heart welled up. "What are you doing? What are you doing? You are killing people." Rabbi Lux screamed, "Enough!"

And at that moment a door swung open in the mind of the rabbi, brass on hinges of iron. He stared out into a space that stretched without time. He saw beyond stars into the planes of night; the realm of black and emptiness. The world was a speck of dust. The horizon extended—farther and farther. At the edge of this stood the rabbi, at the edge of the past of which there is no beginning and the future of which there is no end. He felt the second allotted to him. He felt his breath, life.

The tears dried on Rabbi Lux's face. He shifted in uncomfortable and clammy garments. Shivering, he whispered into the receiver, "Enough. I'm sorry."

Mrs. Blatz hung up. The rabbi went into his bedroom to get some dry clothes. He would go to City Hospital, the morgue, the state insane asylum. He would make rounds. Maybe they had been trying to call him. He was going out the door when the phone rang again.

"I just talked to Simcha Tantzenn! He promised . . ."

"He's dead, Mrs. Blatz! Do you hear me? Dead! Dead! Dead!"

And the rabbi ripped the phone out of the wall.

EPILOGUE

VAUDEVILLE ends happily. Ours is no exception. An epilogue.

The first bit—Rabbi Lux's bowels were destined to improve. Yes—no more sitting for hours on a white enamel seat.

Even happier news of Yehoodiss. More than an hour and a little cut to kill her. She bled a lot—but plenty of juice in her. Thank God—they got to the hospital in time. A few months in a sanitarium, she was as good as new. Where are she and Rabbi Lux now? In Montreal? In Tahiti?

Hudson Bay. A good place to cool off. The rabbinical board has sent him off to a simpler congregation. Somewhere that he doesn't understand the language.

Best—what do you think happened the day after they took Yehoodiss Lux to the hospital? Mrs. Blatz gets a letter. Harvey Blatz is found. He's coming home. From a P.O.W. camp. It's an exchange.

Who found him? Why did they exchange him? *A nudnik.* Who knows? Maybe Simcha Tantzenn.

Columns in the *Boston Globe* and *Herald Traveller.* An article in the *Jewish Advocate.* Headlines in the *Dorchester Record!* Miracles don't happen every day. Especially ones that Simcha Tantzenn is implicated in. This one got full publicity.

Harvey Blatz was a hero. Dorchester found itself with a war hero. Something to show off to the rest of Boston.

Of course, Harvey's credentials had to be checked before the welcoming festivities were organized. There were a few strange facts. For instance, how had he fallen into the hands of the Communists? His unit was at least a hundred miles behind the lines. No one in the Defense Department rushed to pin a medal on his chest. There was muttering from some quarter that he could be disciplined, A.W.O.L.

Jerry Weisberg, commander of our post of the Hebrew War Veterans, conducted a personal investigation. He called up Simcha and told him that before the H.W.V. could begin arrangements for Harvey's homecoming, they wanted a full review of the boy's record.

"Top theecret!" said Tantzenn.

"We got to know," Weisberg insisted. He was a tough nut, a full corporal, Supply, in the Second World War.

"All wight, we'll thend you to Wathington," cried Simcha.

"How . . ." Weisberg began.

"You fwy, govehment expenthe. All awwanged! You thee the thecretary at Defenthe. Athk!"

The word got out immediately. Simcha was sending Jerry Weisberg, *government expense,* to the Pentagon. Jerry was going to speak to the secretary himself. No beating around the bush. Go right into the cabinet and open the drawers to look at Harvey's records. Simcha would pluck one of those strategic bombers with a hydrogen bomb tucked under the wings out of the sky for his errands.

No? How come then, Jerry Weisberg, coming home from his shift at the Morton Street Auto Garage, gets a call at midnight two days later, "We going to pick you up. Weady?"

And ten minutes later Simcha, dressed in Air Force blues with silver eagles staring fierce and bright-eyed from his shoulder blades, arrives in a blue jeep. Cockeyed Zitzz, sporting first-sergeant stripes, bustles out of the front seat. The queer in khakis, airman second on his arm, is behind the wheel. They troop into Weisberg's house.

Jerry has hardly wiped the grease off his hand. On the bed lies the uniform of commander in the Hebrew War Veterans. There are three pounds of medals on the black jacket, all but one ounce earned since leaving the Army and joining the H.W.V.

He is just fastening the top button of the white shirt when the queer, Simcha and Cockeyed grab him. They strip off his shirt and underwear. They truss him in an Air Force jock. And a minute later Weisberg finds himself in front of the mirror in green fatigues. No stripes. He is an airman basic.

"What the f . . ."

Cockeyed Zitzz slams him from behind with a blackjack. They tape his mouth with a roll of black adhesive and carry him out to the jeep.

Commander Weisberg regains consciousness somewhere outside of Boston. On a dark road with tall trees speeding by. He can't say a word. He has to breathe through his nose and it's stuffy.

Are they going to bump him off? He starts to cry.

Tears trickle down on the black adhesive, melt against its sticky surface. Suddenly the queer jams on the brakes. The jeep screams to a stop in front of a lighted gate. Jerry, in front, sees a man with an M-1 come forward. Jerry jumps. Cockeyed Zitzz pulls him down and, shoving him across the seat, sits on him. Weisberg wants to scream. His mouth is bound tight though, full of tar and spit. He hears, "Yes, *sir!* Yes, sir! Straight ahead! Yes, *sir!*" The gates close. He hears them creak, then slam. The jeep roars ahead. Cockeyed gets up off him.

Simcha in the back seat leans forward and smiles, "Welax."

Barreling down a street of bulky warehouses and hangars, the queer abruptly jerks the wheel to the right and they skid on two wheels into the gravel alley between a pair of unlighted quonsets. Smashing against the ringing tin, the jeep bumps a dozen feet and, in front of a small truck, stops. The men get out. A few hundred yards away, out on a runway, a plane is being loaded. The alley, however, is shrouded from view. In the truck a voice calls out from the driver's seat, "Simcha, that you?"

"Wight!"

"Trow him in. I'm gettin' noivous."

"All right," snaps Cockeyed Zitzz. "A moment, we'll be ready. Okay? Get the bag!"

The door of the truck swings open. A small wizened man with stripes on his arm identical to Cockeyed Zitzz's jumps down to the ground. "Don' forget," he says over his shoulder, limping to the back of the van. "A nomber. Oderwoise I dump dis package over a Joisey scrapyard."

"Epstein," whispers Cockeyed Zitzz, "it's sure. Your Air Force I.D. The last three numbers. Send them in."

Sergeant Epstein looked around with a blue pouch of suspicion under his eye.

"A misprint! First time in the history of the *Boston American.* Someone stuck their finger in the linotype. All right?"

From the back of the van, the sergeant pulled a wide, empty blue duffel bag. He beckoned the men over. "Fol' him in two, you goiys. He should fit."

Commander Weisberg looks up at Simcha's grin. "Govehment expenthe!" Tantzenn whistles as Jerry looks into the duffel bag held up by Epstein for inspection and then the whistle snaps in his head as Cockeyed for the second time that night brings down on Weisberg's brains a fat bag of lead. They fold him neatly for his free trip to the Pentagon.

Cockeyed should have hit him again. That lead tranquilizer only carried Commander Weisberg as far as Baltimore. The jet ran into turbulence over Maryland and they had to circle Washington, D.C., for a couple of hours. Jerry awoke in the duffel bag tumbling around in the hold of the airplane. He almost puked in the bag. With his mouth taped, he would have choked to death. Up and down, back and forth, the plane rolled. It was no small trick to keep his stomach down. To the Pentagon! He is bounced from one truck to another, thrown down chutes, kicked into a bin, dragged along the floor, dumped into a sorting machine.

The Russians might look into it. Via Simcha, Jerry penetrated to the heart of the Pentagon. And who should untie the bag and stare down at his bruised face but the secretary.

Miss Myra Ginsburg. Think Simcha cheated? Think the Secretary *of* Defense would have known where to go for the information on Harvey? Ever hear of the mess in Asia? That's how much the High-Ups know about what is where. Miss Myra Ginsberg who calls her mother in Dorchester every night on the Hot Line, knew just where to get hold of anything in the Pentagon.

Of course, Jerry was chagrined he didn't get to walk around and meet the generals. Smoke cigars with the brass. Discuss the latest tactics. He had been collecting advice to give to the President. No, Myra shoved a packet of carbon copies into his hands. He tried to beg her—untie him—get him out of the bag. His mouth was taped. She gave him a nice smile and began to lace the blue duffel's strings together. Pinching his cheek, she hit him with an Air Force eagle, a copper paperweight.

Forget the trip home. After the sorting, it was only an hour or two. Let's rejoin Commander Weisberg refreshed and in the hands of his buddies, who met him in the blue jeep and brought his black uniform so he could ride up in glory to the G & G to breakfast in style. Weisberg hardly had time to read the carbons but he had already found excuses for every objection. Harvey was exonerated.

Anyone who knew the tactics of that campaign knows the lines were shifting. Harvey was ahead of his company, but such an error is commendable. It smacks of leadership. The direction in which Harvey went had been safely in the rear. The enemy suddenly showed up there. "A genius!" shouted Weisberg, the boy had outguessed the experts. If the Defense Department was so full of anti-Semites that they wouldn't give Harvey a decoration, our Hebrew War Veterans would make it up. They struck their own medallion, a silver grenade in the center of a gold Star of David. They would hang it around Harvey's neck. A prisoner of war? Nothing was too good for such a sacrifice as Harvey had made. Other men had gone crazy, been brainwashed, spilled the beans in the enemy camps. No one could make such a charge about Harvey. Just like in Hebrew school, he didn't say a word. That silly smile of his had worked wonders. It threw the Communists into confusion. They sent him home in the first batch with a few generals and VIP's.

Harvey was a hero! We knew that as soon as we saw the photograph of him in *Life* magazine, between the gaunt, drawn faces of the two generals, a crazy grin. He remembered to smile at the little birdie in the camera. Pluck!

Dorchester was beside itself trying to find a suitable expression of gratitude. Two days after the picture in *Life* magazine, the Hebrew War Veterans marched into Franklin Park, followed by hundreds of kids. They dipped the colors by the wall of the old Ape House. A brass plate was nailed into one of the stones.

PRIVATE BLATZ PLAYGROUND

Simcha handed out free ice cream to the children and pinched their little bottoms. They clambered on the wall above his head and swung on the bars.

A hero's welcome was in store. It was unfortunate that Harvey couldn't come right back to Dorchester. He had to be debriefed. He had nothing to say, a short business. Yet he was suffering from malnutrition. Despite the smile, he was a hospital case. He would be coming back to Boston in a litter. They had a bed for him at the veterans' hospital.

Harvey! Harvey! You were scheduled to come into a little military field just outside Boston with no fanfare whatsoever. An ambulance would take you to the veterans' hospital. Would this do?

Tantzenn had offered a private plane to bring Harvey home. The Defense Department despite a High Place plea turned it down.

The regular plane had to be diverted. Or replaced. It was a military emergency. Simcha swung into action.

An order was cut signed by General Ginsburg of the Continental Air Command. It ordered an ancient C-47 diverted from bombing practice at Eglin A.F.B., Florida, and flown to Boston. The plane was to stop and take on a new crew and passengers in Washington, D.C. Another order, signed by the same officer, announced to the Air National Guard unit in Boston that its summer encampment that year would take place in the month of December. The unit was to fulfill a top-secret mission. All papers related to it were classified. No one in the unit had security clearance. Only the orders arrived, requesting a skeleton crew to take available transportation down to Washington, D.C., and stand by at an abandoned runway to take over operation of a mystery plane. Next, arrangements were made with the Pawtucket to Boston airline, which had the use of a tiny strip at Logan Airport, our main terminal, to cancel all flights of its twin-engine Cessna on December 28.

Things were buzzing. The telephone kept ringing at the Hebrew War Veterans post. The Pentagon was calling the G & G.

Harvey Blatz received an honorable discharge. Before separation he was promoted to sergeant. General Ginsberg was ready to cut an order giving him a battlefield commission as captain but . . . wiser heads prevailed.

December 28 was D-day. "Harvey will be home for Chanukah" golden posters up and down Blue Hill Avenue announced. Like candles their yellow DayGlo lit up fences and porches in Dorchester. It was a bigger miracle than the eight-day Menorah. And Harvey was our community's Maccabee. A monstrous Chanukah party at the roller-skating rink was planned for his arrival. The ambulance would stop between Logan Airport and the veterans' hospital for an hour or two. Harvey was to be guest of honor at the party. They would stuff him with enough *kishka* and corned beef to take care of that malnutrition. They would have bathtubs of noodle soup. Simcha printed up 50,000 tickets and sold them in blocks of a hundred to people who wanted favors. A buck apiece! There was only room for 5,000 in the rink. It was the fun of the thing that counted. He got caterers to donate food. Entertainment to come for nothing. The Hebrew War Veterans paid for the use of the roller-skating rink. All the money went to the Blatz Goodwill Fund. Simcha and Cockeyed Zitzz, the two trustees.

On to the day! Logan Airport, a windy, frosty December morning. We're standing in a crowd of shivering dignitaries. Simcha has called up everybody in the Commonwealth and promised them the Jewish vote next election. Every has-been in Massachusetts politics bundles up in a warm overcoat with a bottle of spirits, drives out to meet the plane. Two ex-attorneys general, a former state treasurer, the old mayor of Boston, a host of candidates for the state legislature and city council, a bunch of anxious Italian bookies who've laid odds on the plane coming in, standing at the edge of the big Jewish turnout from Dorchester, Mattapan and Roxbury. It's merry, everyone drinking and swearing, and the plane is an hour late. Simcha is cursing the Air National Guard and threatening the colonel—their next unit encampment will be in Alaska.

Suddenly a dot appears in the sky. It wavers in the air, dipping up and down. As it comes closer, it resembles a drunk. The wings tip first one way and then the other. Veering sharply to the right, it almost crashes into a Boeing jet; turning abruptly to the left, it shears off the tip of a helicopter. Cheers go up from the men in blue through the crowd. It's the C-47 flown by the Boston Air National Guard.

Three reform rabbis go down on their knees to pray for the safe landing of Harvey Blatz. Golden banners, huge balloons, go up, "Happy Chanukah, Harvey!" An 18-foot Menorah rises, blazing, in the midst of the throng.

The siren of the Logan Airport ambulance begins to scream. The C-47 is trying to wiggle into a landing pattern. It's spinning like a *dreidel.* Frantic signal lights are going on and off all over the runway.

A tailspin! The crowd looks up in horror. Too late to run! They freeze and grip one another, praying.

And above the heads of the mob of cowering politicians; their hands over their eyes as the box dives toward them in the gray December sky crisscrossed with the faint beams of searchlights trying to transfix the tumbling structure in a million watts of candlepower; despite the gesticulations of the Air Force colonel (a downtown lawyer), whose windmilling hands are waving his men toward the tower of the Hancock Building as he stands out on the runway attempting to give basketball signals to the crew aloft; despite the screams, the oaths on Simcha Tantzenn as thousands quake and sink into the slush, hearing the buzz of the murderous propellers, nearer and nearer, wind stinging their cheeks; right over the Menorah the plane pulls out of the spin, straightens its wings, circles round, slowing; glides in at the far end of the runway to make a perfect three-point landing.

The plane cuts its engines. There is a moment of silence. And Simcha steps forth. The musicians of the Hebrew War Veterans Band push trumpets, flutes, tubas to their frozen lips and bleat the first notes of the "March of the Vilna Chassidim" to greet Harvey son of

Jacob Blatz. Simcha and three dignitaries, Cockeyed, the queer and Commander Weisberg, step out to be first to welcome the war veteran home. Behind them, the politicians arrange themselves in a receiving line.

The golden candlestick blazes. Its eight candles shoot up against the leaden sky. The doors of the C-47 are rolled open.

Solemnly the cortege of four approach the plane. Mrs. Blatz at the edge of the crowd tries to run forward. Her honor guard, two burly members of the H.W.V., grab the mother's arms and pin them to her side. Rigid, she stands at attention as the siren starts. It wails in time to the band. The siren is on top of a wooden ambulance, an antique, stolen from the garage of the Mattapan Insane Asylum. This vehicle now lurches onto the concrete landing strip, its engine choking with tears, spitting and coughing, it follows the lowered heads of the four, who move forward to take the litter of Harvey Blatz and bear the bruised body. The litter appears at the doorway of the plane. A reporter for the *Dorchester Record* is standing by. His picture will appear next week. A frightening photograph, a bag of wishbones that stare up at the camera. It is no human being that lies on that cot but a frail chicken giblet, one that has had the fat boiled off it. For two weeks, since they told him he was going home, he hasn't been able to eat. There's a tube wired to the sliver they call his arm, pumping sugar, water, vitamins, intravenous.

The crowd would weep if they could see him. Even Simcha, bending over the cot to shake Harvey's hand, is taken aback. All that is left of Harvey is a grin. Simcha smiles back. He licks his lips, quips, "Better late than never! What a thweetie!" And tries to pinch Harvey's cheek. But there's no cheek to pinch, Simcha finds himself grasping a bone.

Turning around, Simcha motions the hospital attendants and the ambulance to follow him. He and his three fellows will carry Harvey to the receiving line. Simcha takes one pole of the litter, Cockeyed, beside him, another. The commander and the queer in back take the other two. The band strikes up the dirge. With measured strides, stern faces, the litter bearers march followed by the ambulance.

The crowd! The frenzied crowd cries out, whoops, raspberries, screams. At the edge of the mob, Mrs. Blatz, blind with tears, bellows like a wounded rhinoceros. And the crowd driven on by this animal shouts to outblast a thousand jet streams. The doors of the hangars shake grass in the wind. Harvey is coming home! The broken body of a hero is being borne to them like the rabbi of Mainz in his basket. And his deliverer, Simcha Tantzenn, who has snatched him out of the jaws of death, pulled him out of a nameless Asian grave to come home and eat potato *latkes*—Simcha is bearing him with his own hands to Dorchester. The world claps itself deaf.

How can Simcha resist? He waves his hand at them. "God wove you!" He waves both hands at them. The cot dips and Harvey rolls off. In the sea of applause he is lost like a bit of flotsam and the ambulance wheels right over his brittle bones breaking them, pretzels under its tire rims.

The cot is hardly lighter. Simcha, his bearers, waving to the crowd, don't notice until they reach Mrs. Blatz. Even blind with tears, she can smell her son. She puts out a hand and gropes on the canvas, screams in Simcha's face, "Where's . . ."

No more! Get Harvey safely to the hospital!

He was picked up and thrown into the ambulance. Its chassis shivering on rusty springs, it sped from the airport, jumping at every hole in the road; rigid shocks, jolting, fracturing nuts, bolts, every bone in Harvey's body left unsplintered. Up and down the streets of Boston the ambulance charged, screeching on one wheel, two; the attendants grinding the siren, searched in desperation for the veterans' hospital. The driver didn't know where it was and there was no time to stop and ask directions. Circling Scollay Square for the third time, they decided to make tracks for Mattapan. The man in back could die on them. There was always a spare bed at the state insane.

So that's where Harvey wound up. In critical condition. He couldn't be moved. They flung him down on a cot in the men's ward and strapped him in as best they could. The doctor who hurried in to see him, swore, above the screams of the patients, if the boy was moved another inch, the spinal cord would snap. He was here to stay until those bones knit.

"Itth a *mechayeh!*" said Simcha to Mrs. Blatz. "You know how far the vetewans' hothpital ith? You got your boy home in Mattapan, a few thtreeth away. Thee him evewy day! And give him a kith fwom me." Yes, Simcha beaming over the tearful mother, transformed everything into a blessing. Who wanted a private room at the veterans'? Wouldn't Harvey like a little company? And Simcha was going to arrange some special things for Harvey. For instance, a telephone right by his bed. Mrs. Blatz could call her *boychik* at any hour of the day or night. If she could hear him over the din, the shouts of his friends.

So let us leave Harvey for good. Actually things are looking up for him. The doctors are looking into that smile of his. His mother calls him every hour to make sure he's still there. He can't move to answer yet. Still, there's always someone who will howl a few words of encouragement into the phone.

As He promised, "My spirit which is upon you and the words which I put in your mouth shall not depart, from your or your children's mouth, or your childrens' children's mouth."

Amen.